# ALIEN'S MATE

## Earth Brides & Alien Warriors

## TINA MOSS

ALIEN'S MATE
Earth Brides & Alien Warriors, Book 2

TINA MOSS
www.tinamoss.com



Cover Design by MilbArt. All stock photos licensed appropriately.

Edited by Danielle DeVor.

For information on subsidiary rights, please contact the publisher at info@tinamoss.com.

2nd Edition. Originally published by City Owl Press.

Print Edition ISBN: 978-1-964370-03-3

Digital Edition ISBN: 978-1-964370-02-6

Printed in the United States of America

# PRAISE FOR TINA MOSS

"*Alien's Captive* delivers steam, danger, and purpose. Filled with enticing world-building and polarizing secondary characters, it's a simple yet tumultuous introduction to this alien sci-fi romance series… Readers who love sexy aliens, death matches, and brave heroines should bypass all checkpoints to book immediate passage on this space adventure!"
— *InD'tale*

"Moss' *Code Black*, a near-future tale of paranormal humans living under the repressive Northern American United Government, chugs steadily along with occasional fireworks… A cast of vampires, psychics, and shape-shifters delivers…witty quips that round out this solid example of the genre."
— *Publishers Weekly*

"*Red Alert* is a superb read for paranormal fans. It is captivating from the first scene, and the fast pacing keeps the reader engaged for the entirety of the novel."
— *InD'tale*

"The introduction to the *Paranormal Crimes Division (PCD)* promises to be entertaining and tense. Humor is never far from the surface, which comes in handy because the world they patrol is treacherous and fear-inducing."
— *RT Book Reviews*

*To my readers of alien pickles, by the stars, you better prepare for this one with a lot of water on hand! Run that cold shower, and hydrate, hydrate, hydrate. It's about to get hot between the...pages. Enjoy!*

# Author's Note

I cannot thank you enough for picking up this book. I want you to feel safe and secure when reading. As such, I've included a list of content information available on my website at: www.tinamoss.com/content-info/

If you have any concerns about the contents of this book, please be sure to check that page first. Thank you again and happy reading!

## Sage

"IF YOU DON'T TURN ON RIGHT THIS SECOND, I'M sending you to the scrap pile." I huffed at the blasted fuel converter. "See how you like being space dust." Clasping the astro-wrench in my fist, I beat it against the machine's outer hull. "I'm warning you." A clip-clip sound was the only response to my threat. "Okay, on three. One…" Another strike from my tool. "Two…" Cranking gears groaned in answer.

"What happens on three?"

The voice startled me from my rantings. I jerked up, knocking my head on the top of the fuel converter. "What the——?"

"Oy sorry." A gentle hand landed on my shoulder and guided me from the infernal machine. "You all right now?"

"Oh, Dr. Harper." I rose from a crouch and wiped stray fuel droplets from my coveralls. "What are you doing here?"

"Apologies for disturbing you while you're working, Lieutenant Kadaran." The good doctor ran a hand through her curly hair. The tight coils sprang forward, framing the doctor's high cheekbones and thoughtful eyes. Her long white lab coat, while not the most flattering, did not derail from her statuesque form.

I sighed, feeling like a goblin in comparison. The fluorescent lights overhead would make me appear ghost-like, but with the doctor's perfectly smooth brown complexion, she was highlighted like a goddess. "Just Sage is fine. No formalities needed." I bit my lip and stamped down the jealousy that bubbled inside me. It wasn't the doctor's fault that I struggled with some insecurities. Having three gorgeous sisters would do that to a girl. "And it's not a worry. How can I help you, Dr. Harper?"

"Please call me, Grace." She smiled with straight white teeth. "Well, I'm afraid I have to remind you about your check-up."

"Now?" I all but whined. The only thing worse than dealing with the moonbase's decrepit machinery was a medical visit.

"Well," the doctor looked around the corridor as if confirming we were alone, "it's been a week since your inoculations and implant. So, I'd like to test that everything is working as it should."

I laughed aloud. "Doc, I'm in no danger of pregnancy. Trust me." Circling the birth control implant under my forearm, I patted it in reassurance. "And I don't feel sick or any side effects from the shots." My grin was lopsided. "Think I'm good."

"Oh but—"

Before the doctor could continue, Taylor, computer genius and best friend extraordinaire, popped into view from the far corner and jogged up to us. Her palms went to her knees as she sucked in several breaths. "I-I..." She struggled to get in air.

"Whoa there, Tay." I patted her back lightly. "You okay?"

"May I help you?" The doctor—no wait, she'd said to think of her as Grace—grabbed a mini-scanner from her pocket and ran it over Taylor from head to toe.

*Whoosh.* The air squeezed out of her. "That was a run." Taylor dusted off her jeans and rose to her full height, coming in several inches below Grace, and yet still a finger's length taller than me. "I'm good, Doctor, thanks." Waving the scanner away and bouncing in her sneakers, she turned her attention on me. "Sage, you won't believe it, but the com signal has gone out on the satellite station again." Her devilish grin lit up her freckled face. "Up for a trip?"

I narrowed my eyes at her. "This wouldn't be like the last time, would it?"

Taylor blew her overly long blond bangs out of her eyes and pouted. "Noooo," her elongated vowel ended with her lips in an exasperated 'O' shape. She threw up her hands as if to emphasize her point. "And you know that wasn't my fault. The computer said the signal was jammed. How was I supposed to know it was a false alarm?"

"Did you double and triple check your readings?" I knew she had. The woman was an absolute savant when it came to anything programmable. Sure I was an engineer and no slouch, but Taylor Wayne lived, breathed, ate, and slept tech. I, on the other hand, loved the mechanical. Give me a machine, and I'd make it work. Then, Taylor would give it life—well, a cyber one.

"Oh so that's how you want to play today?" Narrowing those hazel eyes at me, she waved at Grace. "Dr. Harper, I think you need to take her to the med bay. Clearly, my friend here is suffering from some type of delusional episode."

The poor doctor looked between us as if unsure what to do.

"Don't worry, Grace. She's kidding." I shook a finger at Taylor. "No scaring our doctor. And besides, you've been known to slack off a time or two." That was a complete lie, but riling up my friend was my favorite hobby. And she was so much easier than any of my sisters.

"You!" She spun away and started down the hall. "I'm not falling for your tricks, Sage. You're either coming or you're not."

I glanced helplessly at Grace for backup. Her toothy smile returned, and she shrugged. "You could always still come with me for that check-up."

My mouth dropped open in horror. Clamping it shut, I stared at her. "No offense, Doc, but I'm off!" Chasing after Taylor, I shot like an arrow released from the bow. "Tay! Wait for me!"

THE TRIP TO THE SATELLITE STATION WAS BLESSEDLY short. With my big sister, better known as Captain Jane Kadaran, pulling rank and accompanying our little space flight, the two-seater shuttle was cramped. Since Jane flew and Taylor had called shotgun, I was stuck slumping in the pull down seat behind them.

"Why are you here again?" I said with no attempt to hide my irritation. I loved Jane, truly. But when she barked orders like she owned every corner of the galaxy, I wanted to scream. I didn't begrudge her being in charge. She was an amazing captain and earned her rank through no small trials. However…

"I don't answer to you, Lieutenant." Her midnight blue eyes narrowed as she shot me a look over her shoulder.

That attitude of hers rubbed my patience raw. "Listen, Captain." I sucked my teeth. "Taylor and I have this completely under—"

"Ladies," Taylor interrupted. "As much as I'd love to grab some popcorn for this sibling spat, we have a job to do."

Jane grunted as she steered the ship into the satellite station's docking bay. Killing the engine and opening the hatch, we all shuffled free. I had to push the passenger seat forward on its mechanical wheels to pass through the door.

Taylor's giggle softened her earlier words as she continued where she left off, "Besides I want to hear more about our aliens."

"They're not *our* aliens." I rolled my eyes. Ever since the Rhonar, a species of alien warriors, had made contact a few short weeks ago, all anyone could talk about was them—and their offer.

Jane muttered under her breath but loud enough for me to hear, "They might be."

Latching onto her arm, I forced her to stop in her tracks and look at me. "Say what now?"

"I can't say." She shook me off and continued forward.

"Oh no you don't." I circled around her, arms crossed over my chest. "You're not getting away with that. What do you mean?"

Jane sighed. "Do you know what they're after?"

I huffed. Everyone on the moonbase and Earth knew about the aliens. When the Rhonar first found us, they claimed to have discovered the fate of our lost deep-space flight. We hadn't heard from it in months and feared the worst. As it turned out, we were right to be afraid. The starship had been attacked and the whereabouts of most of the crew were still unknown. Only one survivor had been recovered—saved by a Rhonar warrior.

To say we were skeptical was an understatement, but the holo-vid from the human scientist and member of the deep-space flight, Ava May Kouris, reassured us. Dr. Kouris hadn't been back to Earth yet, but she was already a celebrity. Reproductions of her holo-vid were plastered everywhere with the title, *First Contact Achieved,* in bold letters. Although Earth knew about aliens, only the moonbase personnel understood the gritty details of what they wanted.

"Brides," I choked on the word. As a modern, 22nd century woman, I wasn't ready to be a mail-order bride for some alien species—even if Dr. Kouris' classified section of the holo-vid made it all sound like a fairy tale. I wasn't buying into fated mates and cosmic connections. My feet remained firmly planted on the ground, although I lived in space. But whatever, I was a practical engineer, not a fantasy princess. "And we're compatible."

Then again, after the punctures in the atmosphere, the decreased land masses and minimal availability of livable space on Earth, the diminishing overall population and the vast outnumbering of the female populace, our options were dwindling. I couldn't afford to be a prude about this, if it meant humanity's survival.

"Yes," she said stoically as we headed toward the outer rim of the satellite. "Now that our geneticists have deemed it possible to reproduce—"

Taylor clapped her hands together in mock excitement. "How romantic."

Jane pinned her with a stare.

Taylor gulped.

"As I was saying," Jane continued, waving us to walk and talk. "The Rhonar believe we humans may have evolved from one of their lost colonies. Whether or not that's true, we know we're a genetic match with these aliens. And since the human male population is…"

"Slim pickings," I filled in for her helpfully, a smirk curling my lips.

"Yes." She sucked her teeth. "And the Rhonar have the opposite problem—"

"Hold up!" Taylor interjected. "They don't have women?"

Jane sighed. "Are you both going to let me finish, or should I keep this restricted?"

In tandem, Taylor and I made a zipping motion over our mouths. Then, I wiggled my fingers for her to go on.

"Fine. But one more interruption and this conversation is over." She pinned us with that captain's no-nonsense gaze. "Anyway, this is all being declassified as we speak. Our babbler implants have received a global update to be sure we can communicate efficiently. And the GAN plans to broadcast the Rhonar's offer to the women of Earth."

After the catastrophes on our planet, the world's governments eventually got their acts together and joined forces. It resulted in the Global Alliance of Nations with a panel of elected officials that ran the remaining habitable areas, controlling resources and ensuring law and order. It wasn't perfect but after the barbarism I'd read about in history books, it was probably the best governance humanity had since our existence began.

"So, what do we get in exchange for sending women to be breeders?" I couldn't control my cynicism. Mom said it was my most charming trait. She was biased.

"No one is going to be a breeder, Sage." The good captain transformed back to big sister quickly with that exasperated statement. "And no Rhonar are allowed on Earth or the moonbase. If they're staying," she began to tick items off her fingers, "they have to make their own habitable station, provide us with schematics of their advanced technology, and introduce us to potential alien trading partners."

"Why do we need all that?" Taylor's hazel eyes widened so much they made her appear like a blond owl.

"We're getting in the weeds here, ladies." Jane ran a hand through her hair. It was the exact shade of an acorn and never failed to poof, despite her attempts to tame it.

I secretly envied her hair, although I'd never admit it to her. Mine was a boring flat brown in comparison. Each of my sisters was a beauty in her own right, which made me feel like the ugly duckling sometimes. I mean I loved my full figure. I rocked my curves, and I worked hard at my confidence, but did all my sisters have to be beauty queens?

My mother, a single woman who had desperately wanted kids, adopted the four of us over the course of a year when we were all little. Even though we weren't biologically related, we were as tight as any sisters could be, which meant arguments, jealousy, and competition. But a lot of love too. I'd kill or die for my sisters, no question. And Taylor was an honorary sibling.

But right now… "Jane please stop pulling the captain card." I pointed to the area outside the satellite where I spotted the problem. "There's a clog in the com dish, some space debris, and I'd like to get it fixed and back to the moonbase before I turn thirty."

"Fourty-two days!" Taylor cheered a bit too happily.

"Are you counting down?" I asked, incredulous.

She pinched my cheek. "Of course, my little wizened one. Then you can be an old lady with me."

At four months my senior, Taylor wasn't old, but she loved to tease me. Now, Jane on the other hand…

"Pssh." Jane snapped. "If you two are old, what does that make me?"

Taylor stared at me helplessly.

I shook my head. "Oh no, you stepped right into that. I'm not touching it with a ten-foot pole." At only eighteen months older, Jane and I weren't far apart in age. But she had always taken on the elder sister job with relish. As a natural leader, it fit her.

"Forget it, Specialist." Shaking off the comment, Jane opened the cabinet for the space gear. "Let's get to work."

Leaning toward me, Taylor half-whispered, half-cried. "She used my title!"

"You're fine." I laughed, knowing Jane was just shifting into work mode.

Taylor made a mewling noise but stayed silent thereafter.

I hung back and stared through the satellite station's wide curved windows. The clog in the communications dish didn't look too bad. Once I got out there, I was sure I could fix it fast. A shadow danced in the distance, close enough to make out a triangular outline, but far enough not to see the details.

"Aliens," I said softly. It was still tough to imagine. But there they were, flying just beyond reach. I wondered, not for the first time, what they were like. So far they'd been in negotiations with our top officials, but to my knowledge, no one had actually seen them beyond fuzzy holo-vids. At least, if they had, no one was talking. Our technology wasn't as advanced as theirs. "Guess their DNA is right though." I couldn't believe our government agreed to test reproductive compatibility. But our scientists exchanged samples and both species agreed. We could make babies.

I scoffed. That was the last thing on my mind. I mean I liked kids, but I had plenty of time. No biological clock ticking for me, thank you. I rubbed my forearm absently.

"Here you go, Lieutenant." Jane's voice broke me from my thoughts, and I turned from the window. She had readied my jumpsuit while Taylor procured my toolbox.

I smiled, taking the items from them. "Thanks. This is always my favorite part of the job."

"You do seem in your element out there." Taylor shivered at the space beyond the window. She might work on the moonbase, but the vastness of space was not her jam.

I, on the other hand, loved every bit of it. The wide open and endless sea of space with its speckle of stars ignited my dreams. I might be pragmatic, but I had an active imagination. "I am."

"Then, get it done, sis." Jane gave me a one-armed hug. "And be safe."

I hugged her back and grabbed Taylor with my free arm. A slither of awareness crept along my spine. I squeezed them tighter and glanced over Jane's shoulder. Outside the window another shape sped through the darkness. It didn't appear like the steady triangular ship that patrolled the skies. It had a different feel to it, more…unsettling. It flew deeper in space as if hiding in the depths. If I had not been staring in that direction, I would have missed it. A small part of me wondered if I imagined it.

Not wanting to jinx my mission or worry my sister and friend, I pulled back and put as much confidence into my words as I could. "Let's go for a space walk."

# 2

## Brok

"WHAT IS IT NOW?" I TURNED TO THE DUSTY-ROSE colored florin who had stuck by my side like butra dip on geliva sticks. Worse than my favorite sweet treat from back home, at least that sticky substance had the benefit of tasting good. The florin's presence had no up side. He'd followed me around the space fighter incessantly for many rotations, pushing emotions into me, and only briefly popping between dimensions. The times when he left, I could fade into the void. It called to me, the depth of it, the promise of ending this lonely existence. If I would surrender to it then—

*Chit-chit.* The florin snapped in front of my nose. Its irritation pelted into me, burning inside wherever it landed.

I inhaled, staring into the creature's large black eyes. "I faded again, didn't I?"

A *chittering* affirmation. His fluffy white paws clasped his cheeks while his ears bent backward, tucked against his head. His worry and sadness wafted off him and into me. Likely not an intentional move on his part, but our time around each other had turned the empathic creature into a walking ball of feelings.

If only I had the same luxury.

"I'm all right, little one." I scratched behind his ears that rose a beat at a time until they stood up once more. "I will not succumb."

The ferocity in my declaration did not match my inner turmoil. As a Rhonar male, I was a slave to my biology. Unlike others of my kind, I had passed through the first stage, the hunger, quicker than most. Losing all emotions, and being consumed by an endless, gnawing ache that would not abate, had been difficult. But entering the second stage, the void, was far worse. Fighting against a hole that would never fill, a loss that would never ease, was impossible.

Yet, mercy beckoned. A breath beyond the void shone an answer. The faintest of lights in my internal world of darkness. I knew what would happen to me if I met that tempting call. But how could I resist any longer? How did any of my brathers avoid such a fate without a mate to save him from it?

I didn't know.

The florin's presence had washed into background noise as the void ate at me. Even the discovery of Earth, and

with it the success of my mission, had held no
gratification. I couldn't feel the happiness at the
potential of my brathers being saved, nor bask in the
reassurance that I had served my people. I had grown
closer to the edge during the rotations of isolation on
the space fighter. Without my Rhonar brathers around
me, I'd had no relief from the nightmare.

Now they were here, a handful of space fighters like
mine and a battle cruiser patrolled Earth as we tried to
negotiate with the Terrans for the opportunity to court
mates. Yet, even in the presence of my brathers, the void
lingered.

"What was that?" A flicker of movement through my
fighter's viewer caught my eye. It was the first of
anything that had captured my attention.

The florin projected curiosity. I agreed with his
sentiment.

"Shall we have a closer look?" I asked, maneuvering the
ship toward the enigma. It blipped from sight as if no
more than a distant shooting star. But I knew better.
Certain astral bodies projected such an image, but what
was more common?

*Stealth ships.*

I opened a com channel to the battle cruiser. After my
initial discovery of the blue and green planet, I hadn't
initiated further contact with its inhabitants. That was
Commander Torian's job. And one that I did not envy.
For as much as I hoped for a Terran mate to save me

from the curse of my birth, Earth's government was…complex.

"Hailing BC-1." My fighter's computer repeated the call to the lead ship.

The commander appeared on screen. "Fair meet, Brokdar," he greeted formally. "Good to see you." His purple-rimmed gray eyes held a speck of amusement, a false emotion or a florin projection, as my commanding officer was caught in his own void. "How can we be of aid?"

"Greetings, Commander Tor." I used his nickname in part as he was of my *Brather*—family, not by blood but chosen—and in part to lessen the severity of my next words. "Did you see the flicker in sector twelve?"

The space around Earth had been divided into sectors so as to better patrol and protect it. Now that we had a chance at finding mates once more, we were not about to let it be taken from us.

Not again.

The commander straightened at those words, the skin around his eyes tightening. "No. And our sensors picked up nothing." He leaned closer to the screen. "What did you see, Brok?"

"Could be nothing. An astral body, perhaps." I zeroed in on the sector with the positioning unit on my panel. The commander was correct. Nothing showed on sensors. But although I enjoyed piloting my fighter, I never put too much faith in technology. Better to trust one's senses. "Or it could be a stealth ship."

"Crex," he muttered the curse, pulling up a magnified image of the sector on our shared screen. "All warriors, this is the commander," he said to his ship's com unit. "We have a possible code black. Prep battle stations."

"I'm going in." I didn't wait for his permission and cut the call. I was bucking the chain of command, but the florin's curiosity grew stronger. It led me to believe my suspicions were correct.

Passing the Earth's satellite station, a glimmer of my furry companion's surprise drew my gaze in that direction. One of the small Terrans floated in space and donned strange gear: a dome over their head, thick boots and gloves sealed to an inflated suit, and a cylindrical tank on their back. It seemed they were heading for the large circular structure that they used as a sort of primitive communications array.

"What is that fool doing in space?" I grumbled. As much as I admired the courage of the single female Terran I'd met back on my mission on planet Craxon, the Earth natives were physically weaker than most species. It was easy for them to be injured or worse. "Bah, can't concern myself." I pulled my gaze away from the station. Yet, a strange sensation slithered through my consciousness, a nagging sensitivity I couldn't shake. Having no idea what it was, or what it meant, I felt compelled to keep the station in sight at the edge of my viewer, while steering the ship toward the blip in sector twelve. Nothing appeared again in the darkness, nor on sensors.

It mattered not. I had to be sure.

The florin twittered at me, but I could not decipher his meaning. All Rhonar had translator implants coupled with an innate ability for languages. Yet, the florin species had a unique method of communication, each specific to the individual. Although this florin chose to project feelings over images or words, and stick to his odd utterances, I usually understood him well enough. This time? I had no idea what he wanted. He flit toward the viewer.

*Chit-chit.* He flapped his paws.

"You're worried about a stealth ship?" I went for the obvious answer, thinking his anxiety had to be from the unknown.

*Screech.* An ear-splitting wail ricocheted off the ship's walls as he bounced on his three tails.

"Whoa, little one." His apprehension spilled from him in deep waves, pushing hard against my chest. "Calm yourself."

Spinning around, he ignored me. As he stared out the viewer, I noticed he was watching the Terran station. *That's what bothers him?* I didn't like the tiny Terran floating around in space either, but it was none of our business.

"It's not for us to decide how the Terrans conduct their affairs," I said reasonably. Yet, the earlier sense of... something turned my insides frosty. I shook it off with an iron will.

Casting a cold glare over his shoulder, the florin issued one firm *chit* at me, then went back to staring.

"Fine." I barked. "If you want to allow your feelings to control you, have at it."

That had him bounding around toward me, a fiery glow in the depths of his eyes. Before he could let his tirade run rampant, an alarm blasted.

"Code black detected." The ship's voice confirmed my thoughts at the same time a stealth fighter dropped his covert device and appeared in open space. On its tail, and through a swirling gash in the darkness, a half dozen more fighters and a Versaken battle cruiser, almost double the size of our own, burst forth. "Crex!"

The commander's call broke through my ship's communications and ceased the alarm. "All fighters, alpha formation."

We were outnumbered and outgunned, but we were Rhonar. We would not fall.

Banking my fighter hard to the right, I took position on the edge of the V-shaped formation. Our battle cruiser sat at the middle, serving as the command ship, while our other three fighters filled in the lines. From the corner of my viewer, the Terran station sat perched like a ripe yonac ready to be plucked.

"Drav it all!" I signaled Commander Torian. His face popped on screen, lines creasing his forehead. "What is it, Brokdar?"

"Earth's station." I fought to keep composed with the florin's fear pulsing through the air as biting as frozen rain. "One of the Terrans is outside it."

"Outside?" His brow furrowed further. "How? Why?"

"No idea, but I don't think—"

I didn't get to finish my statement as heavy fire hit the side of my fighter's hull. The shields held, but I was knocked back hard into my seat, and the ship rocked to the side, out of formation. Hurdling across the stars, I grabbed the steering yoke and yanked. The fighter groaned in protest.

My florin friend popped into sight atop my panel, chittering away. He projected an image in my mind, the first he'd sent me, of him disappearing and reappearing.

"You went to your dimension and came back?" I gathered from his message and the fear wafting from him.

He jumped around and his utterances turned happy-sounding.

"Good thinking." I praised him while getting my bearings and preparing the ship to return to the battle.

The viewer displayed my brathers fighting valiantly against the Versaken vessels. Although the enemy had the numbers, we had the speed. Our fighters were lighter, faster, and our commander second to none. As the computer initiated a sequence of checks, I tugged the steering column to the left. And not a second too soon.

A Versaken fighter had broken off from the pack and headed straight for me.

The florin shook at my side. I didn't dare spare him a glance. All my attention, all my focus centered on the viewer and the ship barreling toward us. Targeting my ship's weapons on the enemy vessel, I steadied my hand on the controls. The crexing bastard would be in range in a click.

"Laser rays activated," the ship's artificial voice said as the weapons panel snapped to life.

A few beats more and our ships would be nose to nose.

"So be it." I stood my ground, daring my enemy to crash into me.

Neither of us gave way.

A brilliant glow lit up the darkness of space as our weapons took aim. I expected the head-on assault and had shifted power to the front shields. But at the last beat, the Versaken fighter veered upward. My laser fire hit the underside of his hull. He hadn't taken a single shot at me.

*Why?*

Opening the viewer to a wide angle, I scanned for the enemy. What I found made my blood run cold. It had been long, so long since I had felt. Emotions were the memory of a distant past, too vague and out of reach to remember. But as my heartbeats stilled and the air expelled from my four lungs, a wave of fear crashed over me. The shock of it was too intense for words. Like being hit by a blaster on stun, my entire body locked up.

The florin chittered frantically at me, clearly sensing this emotion running through me.

*I don't have time for this.*

I fought the chaos of this strange state, not remembering how to regulate it or what to do about it. By sheer determination I pushed the feeling aside and spun my fighter around. The enemy was headed for the Terran's station at sonic speed, all its weapons locked on its defenseless prey.

I slammed the fighter's hyperdrive control, racing after the Versaken.

"Come on." I willed the draving ship to catch up. "Come on."

The vessel emerged, slowing to stalk its prey. I was a beat behind. Even at sonic speed I could see the enemy's laser on the side of his ship target the Earth's station. The small Terran crawling along the communications array didn't yet notice.

My insides screamed, a panic overwhelming me like a seismic wave on Meizo Prime. It destroyed everything in its path. The chill that racked my body from it almost knocked me off my feet. I held fast to the controls, willing my fighter to reach the station.

*No.* The word crashed through my brain. But it would not change the truth. I would not make it in time.

The enemy fired.

# 3

# Sage

Noise didn't exist in space. That's what I'd always been led to believe. Yet, I had news for our scientists back on Earth and the moonbase. If an explosion decimated a structure thousands, if not tens of thousands of times larger than you, right in front of your face, you heard it.

The jolt from the impact sent me careening backward. I had been tethered to the station, but with the com dish blasted away to nothing, my line snapped, and I floated in open space. Luckily, my suit had taken the brunt of it, protecting me from injury. But with no way to return to the station, and parts of it crumbling before my eyes like a sandcastle destroyed by a petulant child, I was stuck.

"Jane! Taylor!" My cries into my helmet's built-in communications device went unanswered. The array had been hit hard, but so had a segment of the station. If my sister and best friend had been caught in the blast…

*No, no, no. We're not going there, brain.*

I sucked in a breath to quiet my rapidly beating heart. Panicking would not help me out of this mess. "Think," I said aloud. The sound anchored me to the present. "Oxygen check."

"Sixty-four percent and dropping six percent per minute." My suit's internal computer reported the readings.

*Not good.* At that rate I had around ten minutes of air left. Something must have been damaged in the blast. "Initiate maintenance sequence." It would take the system under a minute to analyze, then I'd know what I was dealing with.

Unfortunately, I didn't have that long. A spaceship that appeared as mean as a hornet with a similar body shape rose before me. Slick mechanical arms shot from the sides ready to grip me in their clutches. My gloved fingers grasped the astro-wrench strapped to my thigh. I held it up as if to ward off the terrifying arms that cut through space as easily as a laser.

"Stay back," I screamed inside my helmet.

It was no use. As the arms came within inches of my waist, two things happened at the same time. Another ship, a Rhonar one I'd seen patrolling Earth's space, crashed into the side of the foreign craft. The impact knocked the ship and its grabby arms into the distance.

The second thing was my suit's computer finished its analysis.

"A hole has been detected in main oxygen canister." The robotic voice grated my ears as my breathing grew shallow. "Repair cannot be rendered at this time. Auxiliary tank depleted. Recommend immediate disengagement."

"Thanks." I snarled at the computer. Punching in my com line, I tried to hail the alien ship. "Rhonar vessel. This is Lieutenant Sage Kadaran of Earth's moonbase. I'm in need of assistance."

*There. Calm. Professional.* Who said I couldn't handle a crisis? My stomach twisted, my palms sweat, and I had a funny feeling I'd throw up soon. Whether that happened before my air ran out or not, well that was the gamble.

No answer came through the com line.

"Rhonar vessel," I tried again. "Do you copy?"

Static. Nothing but static. I didn't check the time on my remaining oxygen, but my pulse was rising fast. *Okay. Universal signs here, Sage.* Maybe our tech wasn't compatible. That didn't mean I was out of options. Grasping my astro-wrench tight, I stretched my arms and legs as long as they would go, and then waved my arms back and forth. The tool gave a few more inches in length to my short stature. I didn't know how well these aliens could see, especially from their ships, but I had to catch this one's attention. If I didn't…

*Don't think like that.*

My breaths puffed from my mouth with the exertion. I was using up precious air. "Come on! You're supposed to be some alien superheroes. Can't you recognize the heroine in distress here?"

"Three minutes of oxygen remaining. Advise a resupply."

I sucked in a harsh inhale as if I could hold it on retainer. "Not helping, computer."

The alien ship rotated toward me while I continued to wave at it. Resting as silent as a sentinel in the darkness, I had no idea if the pilot aboard could see my movements, and even if they did, I had no way to make my intentions clear.

"Two minutes of oxygen remaining. Advise a resupply."

*Please understand.* Perspiration slid along my neck and down my collarbone. The tank top I wore underneath my suit stuck tight to my ribcage. I swallowed the acid reflux.

"One minute of oxygen remaining. Advise a resupply."

*I'm going to die out here.* Tears stung my eyes. I shouldn't have gotten mad at Jane. And I needed to stop teasing Taylor so much. I didn't spend enough time with my younger sisters. Hell, when was the last time I called my mom? *I want to hear her voice.* As the last remnants of oxygen spilled into my helmet, regrets filled my heart. I stuck my astro-wrench against my thigh and squeezed my eyelids closed, as if shutting out the truth.

"I don't want to die," I whispered. A wave of dizziness consumed me along with a strange sense of euphoria.

The last voice I heard was the computer. "Oxygen depleted."

Then, everything went black.

## BROK

The battle raged on. I'd struck the Versaken fighter with enough force to send it spiraling from the sector. But not before he blasted the Terran's communications device, and with it, a part of their satellite station. The destruction was evident in the debris clogging up space.

Yet that was not my main concern.

"Where is the Terran?" I grabbed the steering column and rotated the viewer.

*Chit-chit.* The florin bounced toward the right and pointed his paws at the corner of the screen. The agitation coming off him matched my own turbulent… feelings. I still could not believe the sensations crawling inside me, hot and cold in tandem. It made no sense. I hadn't escaped the void, yet the emotions were there, spiraling like a nebula.

I banked the ship where the florin indicated and spotted the tiny Terran. An invisible weight lifted off my hearts. The backs of my knees hit the pilot's chair, and I slumped into it. The Terran was waving their arms, something clasped in hand.

"What is this?" I said to no one in particular. Although, the florin angled his head at me. I rubbed my chest as if to dislodge this inner turbulence. "Why do I feel such relief at seeing this Terran?"

The florin jumped on my chest. His long feet held him steady as his gaze bore into mine. A twittering vibration emanated from between his teeth.

"I don't understand." I scrubbed a hand across my neck. A bombardment of images flitted to me: a forest with crimson leaves and gray trees, thick black dirt, emerald green waters, and a purple mountain range. The florin burrowed into my mind. I swatted at his hide. "There's no time for whatever this is."

Rising from my seat, he scuttled off. He chittered louder than ever as he returned to his normal spot atop the console. I ignored him. The Terran was floating in space unaided. My brathers continued to fight the enemy. I needed to focus on my duty, not whatever had shifted inside me.

I aimed the ship toward the Terran and opened the bottom hatch. With expert precision, I eased the compartment around their body. Maneuvering my fighter, I scooped them up as if it was my own hand plucking them from space. The hatch closed, sealing them inside.

"Engage autopilot." I set the coordinates to hold my position and alert me if any enemy fighters came in range. I had to get back to the battle, but first, I needed to check the condition of my new passenger. I extended my forearm to the florin. "Are you coming?"

His tales flicked and his whiskers tweaked in evident exasperation, but he perched atop my arm. *Chit-chit.*

"Sure. Same to you then." We headed down the metal stairs to the lower compartment.

The Terran laid in the center of the floor, curled on their side. With the seal in place, they no longer needed their odd suit. I knelt beside them to convey this information, marveling at how truly small these beings were, only to discover two startling facts. The Terran was unconscious…and female.

"Med kit," I said to the florin, shaking him off my arm. He scooted to the back wall where the supplies were held. As quick as I dared I stripped the female of her inflated suit, easing a large canister off her back and a strange weapon strapped to her thigh. Although I didn't know her natural coloring, her skin had a tint to it that seemed off. Her chest, covered by a thin shirt, was eerily still.

The florin returned, dragging a kit that rivaled him in scale.

"Thank you." Popping the lid, I scoured the interior for the aid I needed. The oxitube had a single shot of an oxygen rich agent which could revive a fully grown Rhonar warrior. I took another look at the petite female, set the device to a quarter the dose, and injected it. The full gasping breath from the lovely Terran was the most perfect sound I'd ever heard.

I sat on my haunches and stared at her round face as color rose to her cheeks, a slight pinkish hue. Her hair was tied at the top of her head in a tight coil. She appeared similar to the Rhonar females from my memory, but smaller, so much smaller. When standing, she'd likely not even rise to my breastbone. The other Terran I'd met had been tiny too.

*Could it be they're all so small?*

Still this female had an undeniable beauty to her. The rich brown shade to her hair was almost as dark as my own. Her nose was upturned and pert, giving her a mischievous appearance even in slumber. It made me smile. Her lips were full, lush, and begging to be kissed, which had me grinning for a different reason. I glanced down her body. A strange blue material with two straps crossed over her shoulders covered her to her ankles. Yet, it could not hide her feminine shape. Her curves were the stuff of dreams. Too easily I pictured my callused palms holding handfuls.

A sudden gasp dragged my gaze to her face once more. Her eyelids snapped open, and it was my turn to suck in a breath.

"Green," I said aloud. The color of her irises matched the hue of a Dajarian crystal when starlight shone through it. Those light green eyes with their darker ring around the outer edge captured my senses. Without thinking, I reached a hand toward her cheek.

She flinched away. "Who are you?"

"I'm—" Before I could answer her question, the fighter's alarm sounded a high-pitched wail.

The ship's artificial voice confirmed the worst. "Enemy ship approaching."

"Come with me." I hauled the tiny female to a standing position, and half-dragged, half-carried her up the stairs.

"Wait!" She clasped onto my waist, but didn't stop moving. "Where are we going?"

"We need to strap in." Bursting into the control compartment, I pushed her gently into the passenger seat.

"Whoa," she breathed, her eyes bulging as she stared out the viewer.

Taking advantage of her distraction, I used the time to crisscross the belts over her chest and torso and lock her into place.

"Hey!" She slapped at my hands as if realizing my intent. "What are you doing?"

It was too late to fight me now, even if she had stood a chance. She was immobilized to the seat, but the panic in her eyes had me answering. "You see that?" I pointed to the enemy fighter bearing down on us. "That ship is about to attack."

"But…" Her gaze scanned space, locking on the debris. "W-why are they after us?"

That was a good question, but one I didn't have time to entertain. "Later," I mumbled, strapping into the pilot's chair and readying weapons.

The fighter didn't approach, holding its position about a hundred yaunas away.

"He's just sitting there." The female gripped her straps.

She was correct. My gut churned. The enemy had no reason to wait. I engaged the computer. "Scan his ship for weapons." I moved in a few yaunas. The florin scurried up the control panel, and the female screamed.

"Wh-what is that?" Those beautiful eyes of her eyes widened while the florin bounced in front of her. "You're quite a cutie, aren't you?" As she rubbed under the florin's chin, the creature began to purr. "Aww, you're kind of like a dog mixed with a fox…well, with three tails." She laughed as said tails flicked behind him.

"Florin," I said, a bite of jealousy lacing my words. "You need to strap in as well or pop off."

A chitter of annoyance was aimed in my direction, then a soft hum at the female. He patted her shoulder with his paw before he popped out of our dimension.

"Ah?" The female tilted her head to the side. "What just happened?"

"Scan complete." The ship's analysis cut off any response. "Target has three astropoid devices, twelve-hundred rounds of laser fire, and an unknown projectile device."

"Unknown?" I skimmed the readouts. "Traces of aracon particles. What are they up to?"

An eerie stillness pervaded space as if the battlefield was a sentient giant holding its breath.

"I don't—"

The female's words were interrupted by a cacophonous boom. A blinding white light erupted before us, overtaking every segment of the viewer. It lasted a heartbeat before a swirling mass took its place.

"Crex!" I slammed the steering column hard, willing the thrusters to engage.

A squeak drew my gaze to the Terran beside me. "Is that a-a…"

"Yes," I said, unable to hide the grim reality. "It's a wormhole."

The ship lurched forward against my control. Everything in the vicinity, which was us and the debris from the earlier explosion, began to jerk toward the sucking cavity. The enemy ship was no where in sight.

"Hailing all ships, this is F1." I held the broadcast button, sweat trickling beneath my palm. "The enemy has used a projectile weapon to create a wormhole." My voice lowered, heaving with gravel. "I cannot break free."

I opened the com channel to receive a message from any of my brathers. But with no response and the wormhole drawing us closer, I had no hope of them coming to our aid. Even if they had gotten my distress call, no one would be able to get close enough now to free us from the vacuous pull.

I turned to the female. The fear in her gaze tugged at my hearts. I took her hand delicately in my much larger one. She gave me a small frightened smile and wrapped her fingers around mine. Silently, I prayed to Celestia, a devotion that I had abandoned long ago. But if even a chance remained that the sacred divine would protect this tiny Terran, then I had to try.

As the ship began to buckle under the weight of the suction, my life's memories flitted before my eyes. I held fast to the image of this sweet female's face. And I regretted only one thing.

I hadn't asked her name.

# 4

# Sage

DON'T FREAK OUT. DON'T FREAK OUT. THE astronomical willpower it took not to scream was more than I had in me. I let loose an ear-shattering cry as the ship tossed and spun in the center of the wormhole. It was worse, so much worse than all my g-force training on Earth.

"Terran," a rough gravelly voice drew my attention.

As we kept rolling, I struggled to focus on the alien beside me. His eyes were as black as space with a striking silver around the rim. I had the impulse to reach for him, but I didn't dare release my grip on the straps that bound me to my seat. Absently, I realized he must have saved me after my oxygen depleted. *Too bad, we're about to die now.*

"We will get through this," he said as if reading my thoughts. "Just stay with me."

The pressure increased. My brain felt too tight for my skull. The straps dug into my body as every inch compressed into the seat. *Don't faint.* I pulled in tiny sips of air as I labored against the invisible elephant sitting on my chest.

"Almost," the Rhonar's words were strained, as he too fought the wormholes pull, "over."

What felt like an eternity later, we emerged into open space. Nausea hit hard and fast. I didn't dare move—not that I could with the alien harness around me. The top pieces dug into my chest. I squirmed as much as the restraint would allow. "Can you let me out of here, please?"

The front console lit up red. "I'd love to, tiny Terran, but we have an issue."

"Seriously?" I snorted. The ship had been flung through an artificially made wormhole, after the satellite station had been attacked, the com dish blown to pieces, and I'd been stranded in space. I mean, how much worse could it get?

Alarms blasted through the ship. A planet appeared on the viewer at least twice the size of Earth. It's blackish-purple, emerald, and crimson patches did not look inviting. And we were way too close for comfort.

*Had to jinx it, didn't you?* I silently cursed myself.

"We're being drawn in by the planet's magnetic field." The Rhonar warrior pushed at the buttons, one after the other. But the console stayed stubbornly red, and the alarms didn't abate.

"Engines offline." The ship's voice had a metallic quality that burned my already fried nerves. "Impact in five clicks."

"How long is a click?" I asked the alien, not sure if I wanted to know the answer.

His face was grim. "Not long enough."

"Figures." Pushing free a deep exhale, I fought for calm. *Okay, so let's use the time and think this one through.* I ran down a checklist in my mind, the kind I used when solving an engineering puzzle. But I was a bit out of my depth. For starters, I had no idea where we were after being thrown through a flipping wormhole. Add to the list that I was on an alien ship with no time to study its technology, and we were likely crash landing on an unknown planet, and well, I hadn't exactly prepared for this type of situation.

The Rhonar warrior unstrapped himself from the pilot's chair and stood.

I craned my neck…a lot. "Whoa. That's a bad idea."

"No," he said with an air of authority in his tone. This was a man, well male, used to being obeyed. It did things to my body that was entirely inappropriate given our situation. "I should have done this before." He knelt beside me, which still didn't put us at eye level. He was that tall. Bowing his head, he captured my gaze with his. "What's your name?"

"Sage," I breathed. His body jolted for a moment, but his eyes stayed locked with mine. The intensity of his stare was piercing. His expression, so serious yet full of emotion, captured me. I could drown in the depths of that look.

"Say-jah," he repeated, drawing out the syllables like a benediction. "Yes, it fits. I am Brokdar. Or Brok." He smiled, lush lips turning his allure downright dangerous. "It is my honor to meet you."

I hummed. *Brokdar…Brok.* Both fit him too. For a heartbeat I pretended that everything was fine, that I could enjoy this alien encounter at my leisure. I took in his cut jaw and thick brows. I admired his broad, flat nose, and penetrating eyes. His skin was a dark bronze, thicker and tougher looking than a human's. His long black hair was lush, almost feminine, but did nothing to detract from his strength and purely masculine appeal. He'd tied those strands at the nape of his neck. His shoulders were covered in an armor that seemed sturdy yet flexible and ran down his chest and torso. His arms were bare, laden with silvery-black tattoos that gleamed like metal. Tight black leather-like pants left little to the imagination. I jerked my gaze up.

It figured that I'd find the most attractive male in existence to be an alien while subsequently hurdling toward our doom.

"One click to impact," the ship's computer informed.

And there it was. Reality hitting me smack in the face. "You don't happen to have an escape plan, do you?" I hated how small my voice sounded. My chin angled toward my chest. I stared at my fingers as I twisted them together.

Roughened hands yet with such a gentle touch laid over mine, stilling my movements. He bent lower. "Look at me, Sage."

I gulped. This male was impossible to deny. If we weren't about to crash that thought would probably send me running. My track record with alpha males was shaky at best...and miserable at worst. *Not the time.* I met his eyes reluctantly. I wasn't sure what I was asking, but I heard myself murmur, "Yes?"

"All will be well." His grip was firm on mine but he squeezed so carefully. "I vow to protect you with my body and blood." His fist thumped the center of his chest. "No harm shall befall you lest I have fallen. You are safe in my care."

I couldn't breathe. Bound to the seat, I had no ability to move toward him, but somehow it felt like I was sinking into him. His eyes glowed with a silver light in their dark depths. I wanted to fall into those shimmering pools.

As his unwavering scrutiny held me captive, the symbols on his arms glowed. The ship accelerated. Brok shifted behind me, his grip going tight around me like steel bands over the harness. A shining blue light extended from his tattoos, a ball of energy that encapsulated us like something out of an anime.

I didn't have time to consider the magic of it as on the viewer the strange planet grew impossibly larger. This time I didn't even try to stifle my scream.

## BROK

The unknown planet's atmosphere sucked us in, causing the ship to gain speed on the descent. My fighter was built tough, but I had no delusions. The impact would be brutal.

"Hang on," I yelled over the roar of grinding machinery. Pushing my abilities to the limit, I strengthened the energy shield around us.

A crimson and gray forest came into view and beyond it a deep purple mountain range. *Not the mountains.* I beseeched the cosmos in silence, hoping Celestia listened. *Let this female live, and I'll never doubt again.* Drav, I'd travel to the nearest temple and bend a knee to the scared divine, if she granted this boon. My arms burned from the exertion. *I beg you.*

The mountains grew critically close. Yet, a sliver of hope shone to the east, a large pool of green-blue waters. "Ship, hard right."

The jerking motion made me tighten my grip on Sage as the ship grappled to turn. I had little time to suck in a breath and brace before the fighter spun and hit…water. The fighter skidded along the surface, then dove under. It slid along the bottom, the water slowing the impact. Yet, the pool must have been inclined on the far shore as we sprang up midway, the ship's nose and upper half sticking above the water.

"Holy shit," Sage yelped. "I don't even believe it. We're alive."

I shared her disbelief. For us to survive a crash like that intact? The odds were nearly insurmountable. I saw plans to thank the stars and kiss the feet of a Celestia statue in my future. *Thank you.*

"Ah, Brok." She patted my arms that were still locked around her. "I think you can let go now. And I'd really like to get out of this harness."

Every instinct rose to high alert as reality set in. Although we were on a planet who knew where in the universe and had about a million tasks we needed to do to survive, the undeniable truth hit me. I'd found my true mate. Her spoken name had been the key to unlocking the mystery. Even now the void that had haunted me for so long filled to bursting with emotion, with life, with her. I wanted to shout to the skies, but something told me to tread carefully with my sweet Truxoria. As a Terran, she wouldn't understand the Rhonar mating bond, at least not right away.

"Of course." I swallowed hard and drew back my energy. My katra glowed from my shoulders to midforearm, demanding completion of the bond and my mate's symbols to forge on my wrists. I felt my life's blood, my kedara, sing with desire and grow hot. I had fought many battles, been through more than my share of war, but pushing back the mating instinct was perhaps my toughest challenge yet.

Her head tilted to the side, her eyes widening, as I circled around to release her straps. My fingers skimmed over her torso and the side of her breast. She gritted her teeth.

"Apologies, targana, I'm trying to get you free. It's dug into you." It was the truth. I wouldn't take advantage of my mate. Yet, I could not deny that I wanted to touch her, to know her. First, I had to protect her—even from myself.

"What's a targana?" Her penetrating eyes glowed under the ship's emergency lighting.

My mate had a sharp mind. I'd sensed that from her earlier questions. "A nickname of sorts." I had no desire to tell her the truth as it would reveal the depth of the feelings swirling through me. As best as I could translate, it would mean something like "small sweetness" in her language. I doubted she'd appreciate it.

She huffed. "You know that's not an actual answer, right?"

I grunted as the straps released.

Her answering snort of amusement lightened the tension. "That's not either. But I'll let it go." She rose and stretched her arms high. As I predicated, the top of her head began at the bottom of my breastbone. It roused all my protective instincts. She twisted as if checking she was in one piece, and then slapped her thigh. "Um, I'm assuming you took off my spacesuit. But what happened to my astro-wrench?"

My brows pinched together. "Aster-reech?" I had trouble wrapping my tongue around the word, and my translator implant couldn't quite decipher it.

"Yeah, it's the tool I was using to work on the com dish." Her hip cocked to the side, a hand planted on her curvy waist. "It's kind of my good luck charm."

I didn't quite understand what she meant, but I headed toward the lower compartment where the florin had stashed her belongings in a container unit. "This way."

"So, any ideas where we are?" She bounced on the balls of her feet as she walked.

I glanced at my Truxoria. Her pert nose wrinkled as if in thought. "Not yet, but once we retrieve your talisman, we'll assess."

She laughed and the sound slid along my spine, firing my nerves. How would I possibly resist her? The mating fever already swam in my blood, hot and thick. "It's not quite a talisman, but it has gotten me through some tough spots."

"I see." My battle ax held similar meaning for me. Tucked inside the pilot's side compartment, I'd retrieve it and strap it to my back when we finished here. Only with it at my side did I feel whole.

"Not a talker, huh?" A spark gleamed in her beautiful eyes.

I looked over my shoulder as I opened the container unit. A nagging ball centered in my gut. "Would you prefer if I was?"

"Nah." She smiled, and it lit up my world. "I can talk enough for both of us. No worries."

A smirk pulled at my lips. I grabbed her belongings and retrieved her lucky tool. When I held it out to her, she squealed.

Snatching it from me, she held it against her chest and pet it like an animal. Her voice turned odd as she said, "My precious."

"Does it mean that much to you?" I watched the encounter in fascination.

She laughed again, and stars, I'd do anything to hear that sound for the rest of my days. "It's important to me, but that expression is from this super old holo-vid. They called them movies a long time ago. And well, I love this thing."

"Oh." My Truxoria was full of mysteries I'd enjoy unraveling. But now was not the time. We needed to get off this planet. "Come. We have work to do." I held out my hand to her.

Staring at my open palm for a beat, she wrapped her fingers around it and shook it up and down. "Okay, partner. Let's go."

I relished the feel of her smaller hand in mine as I guided her up the stairs. Her skin was soft, but not delicate. Her fingertips had a rougher texture that proved she used them for manual work. She was not pampered then. I'd enjoy spoiling her even more for it.

"Ship, run a full diagnostics and determine where we are." I guided her to the passenger's seat as I took the pilot's chair. She eagerly roamed her fingers over the console. Not pressing anything, but clearly assessing each button. I'd value her help. We needed information, but maybe there was an easier way. "Florin!"

Her head spun in my direction. "Why are you shouting?"

"The creature you met before is a florin."

She tilted her chin forward as if waiting for me to continue.

I sighed. Communication was not my strength. "They're inter-dimensional beings. The Rhonar made an agreement with them."

"Which was?" She prompted.

"They help us manage our lack of emotions, and in turn, we provide them with energy they need."

"Okay." She pulled her legs from beneath the console and folded them under her. The motion gave her more height as she knelt in the seat and leaned over the control panel. "That's a lot to unpack right there. And I so want to hear more, but maybe we should worry about that first." Pointing at the viewer, she muttered, "Haven't I met my chaos quota for the day."

I followed her finger and stared through the screen. "Crex." A creature half the size of the ship stood on the shoreline, staring at us. Its hide was covered in splotchy brown scales. Short limbs were tipped with long claws. Giant black fangs ran along its mouth. The howl that broke deep in its throat shook the ship. Its black eyes fixed on my mate.

My kedara surged forth, igniting my blood. I ripped the door of the pilot's storage unit off its hinges and grasped my battle ax. The symbols of my katra glowed, the blue light brightening the panel.

"Stay inside." I commanded before heading for the exit. My hand slapped the door controls.

Sage called from the passenger seat. "Wait. *You* stay inside. It can't get us in here."

As if in answer, the beast charged toward the ship. Whether it could break through or not was irrelevant.

Nothing threatened my mate.

# 5

# Sage

THE ALIEN HAD LOST HIS MIND. THAT HAD TO BE THE explanation for Brok to leave the safety of the ship and fight that…thing. I patted my astro-wrench at my thigh.

"Well, you can't just sit here and let him face it alone, right? Get moving," I said aloud to bolster my confidence and jumped up from the chair before I lost my nerve. Spotting the exit he had used, I slapped my palm against the door panel as I'd seen him do.

"Access denied." The ship informed me with an inflection in its tone that hinted at snootiness.

I didn't like it. "Oh yeah?" Shaking my tool at the invisible artificial computer voice with one hand, I picked off the covering of the control panel with the other. "We'll see about that."

The interior was constructed of thin multi-colored tubes. "Energy distributors, maybe?" The mechanism appeared different than the technology on the moonbase, but luckily, universal principles applied. *Just have to figure out…* I chewed on my bottom lip. "There!" Pinching the white tube inward with my astro-wrench and tweaking a configuration cap on the green one, the door slid open. "Score a point for me."

I didn't have long to celebrate. Tension swam through the air thicker than the fuel that powered our old, dilapidated moon-rovers.

Not ten yards from the ship, Brok stood with his feet braced shoulder width apart. He held his battle ax in both hands at the ready. The weapon was longer than his torso and had a double-bladed edge. A blue light glowed from his forearms, the same energy that had shielded us during the crash. If I hadn't been so worried, I'd be drooling over him. He was like a fantasy character come to life.

"Okay. No more of that." I tugged on my coveralls, tightening the straps. "You can do this," I whispered encouragement to myself but hesitated beside the ship.

The creature hissed from a mouth laden with fangs. Spit dribbled between its teeth and over its massive jaw. Its hide was covered in muddy brown scales with patches of a sickly greenish hue between them. Although its arms and legs were short, it had six limbs altogether and had to be at least twice the size of Brok. And since the Rhonar warrior kissed the seven-foot mark, it meant the beast was massive.

Since I barely passed five-feet, my gaze traveled up and up to see the top of the creature's head. *And of course it has a spiky mohawk. Perfect.* To say I felt like a guppy caught in an alligator's territory was an understatement. This monster's hide rivaled that of a tyrannosaurus. I liked dinosaurs and all, but in books and holo-vids, not in real life. And definitely, not some alien lizard-dinosaur hybrid straight out of my sci-fi nightmares. *Ugh. Dinozard. Creepy.*

"I told you to stay inside the ship," Brok growled without ever taking his eyes off the beast.

*How did he—* My thoughts halted as the stand-off broke.

Quicker than I imagined possible, Brok launched high in the air while the dinozard charged forward. His ax grazed the creature's mohawk, trimming it to the root. A piercing howl rent the air. I clasped my hands over my ears. The beast snapped its powerful jaws over its shoulder as Brok landed on the middle of its back. A tail riddled with spikes I hadn't even noticed before whipped into a frenzy. The dinozard bucked, trying to dislodge the intruder. Brok held firm, slamming his ax between the beast's shoulder blades.

The wail of rage that broke forth made the creature's prior howl seem tame. It shot upward. Its four hind legs stomped the ground. Brok's ax tore free of the dinozard's back, and he plunged to the side to avoid the creature's wrath. Landing on the blackened dirt, Brok rolled as the beast's fangs clamped down. Yet before the warrior could get his feet under him, the dinozard snapped repeatedly, forcing Brok to continue rolling to avoid that deadly bite.

Frozen by fear, I urged my feet a step forward. Brok needed to get up if he stood a chance of defeating the monster. But while the dinozard's attention remained on trying to chomp the warrior in half, Brok wouldn't stand a chance.

"Okay, Sage. This is it. Do or die." I had to cause a distraction. A hysterical snicker bubbled forth. At least I was good at that. "Over here!" I shouted at the beast. Gripping my trusty astro-wrench tight, I flailed it around like a flag. "Come and get me."

The dinozard's sharp coal eyes zipped to me. "Shit." I hadn't expected it to work quite *that* well. Without thinking, I spun and took off. Sprinting as fast as my legs would carry me, I cursed as I headed toward the opposite end of the shoreline. A forest of gray trees with crimson leaves rose before me, densely packed and ominous. *Better than being eaten.*

Snorts and grunts followed too close behind for comfort. I didn't dare look back.

Diving for the trees, I wrapped my arms around the nearest trunk, using my tool as leverage, and reached for a branch. I hoisted myself up, thanking my baby sister for forcing me to go rock climbing with her. Betting on the dinozard's limbs being less than optimal for an ascent, I hauled ass higher up the tree. With the creature breathing down my neck, I didn't have other options.

The clack of jaws echoed behind me. I pushed my body to move faster.

A rage-filled roar shook the trees. Slowly, I turned my gaze to the ground. What I saw had me hissing through my teeth. The dinozard stood on its hind legs at the base of the tree, digging its claws into the trunk to attempt the climb. That alone should have frightened me, but the creature behind it stole my breath. It had to be Brok, but he looked like something out of a holo-game. His eyes gleamed with a silver light. His muscles swelled, beads of sweat glistening on his skin. His hair had come undone, likely while chasing down the dinozard, and hung wildly around his face. He was covered in dirt from head to toe, but it did nothing to take away from his appeal. He appeared like an avenging angel on the edge of the woods.

"Stay away from her," he bellowed at the beast. But the dinozard had found easier prey and kept pawing at the trunk.

I shrieked as it gained traction, scraping a claw at me. Swiping my astro-wrench at it seemed only to make it more determined to climb.

Brok's face filled with fury, the blacks of his eyes overtaking the silver. Blue energy radiated from his arms and surrounded his body. He threw himself at the beast with such force, it rattled the ground. The dinozard shook from the impact. But it got to its feet too quickly. It snarled, charged, and bounced off the energy shield. Brok wielded his ax, swinging the weapon in wide arcs.

The two circled each other, each searching for an opening.

I placed my astro-wrench back in my thigh strap and clung to the branch supporting me as the two fought below. If I fell, I'd survive but not without injury. And if the dinozard got a hold of me? *Not a good idea.* I hugged the tree limb tighter.

Without warning, the beast rushed Brok again. This time it used its thick skull to ram against the energy shield. The Rhonar grunted and held his ground. Yet, an inch at a time, the dinozard pushed until the shield flickered. Swinging furiously, Brok tried to land a blow on the beast's softer underbelly. But each attack caused the energy to dissipate further. And the dinozard dodged the strikes.

"Crex you!" Brok pulled a knife from his boot, launching it at the creature. He nicked the underside at last, but not enough to stop the beast.

The dinozard roared again. It swept Brok's legs from under him. Yet, instead of continuing the attack, it spun around and headed straight for my tree. My eyes widened as the beast slammed head first into the trunk. The branch underneath me snapped. I cried out in shock as I plummeted toward the ground.

"No!" I heard Brok's pained shout, but he was too far to help me.

I grabbed wildly for purchase, my fingers bleeding from the attempt. But it all happened so quickly, I couldn't gain a solid grasp. Tucking my body into a ball, I did my best to prevent injury. I squeezed my eyes tight, not wanting to see the end. When I landed, I felt the breath knock from my lungs. Yet I hadn't fallen as far as I expected. I put my hands tentatively beneath me to discover a strange texture. I opened my eyes. "What the hell?"

The monster laid beneath me. Whether it had knocked itself unconscious from striking the tree or it was the impact from my fall, the beast was out cold. I'd hit his scaly head and now slid part way down his back. The slice where Brok's ax had struck earlier oozed black blood. The liquid coated the bottom of my coveralls. "Ewww."

"By the stars," Brok breathed, hooking his weapon to his back. "You must be the luckiest Terran in the universe."

His wicked smile turned my cheeks hot. He bent over the beast and scooped me off its back. His arms were as hard as iron. His chest, covered in his armor, radiated heat. An answering fire stirred inside me, igniting my senses. My pussy clenched. *Oh no. No, no, no.* I was not about to get horny in the middle of absolutely no where with a big bronze alien. *Nuh-uh.*

I tilted my face towards his. My voice was more than a little huffy as I said, "I can walk, you know."

"That is not wise." He raised a dark brow at me, then motioned toward my leg with his chin.

Three nasty-looking claw marks ran across my right calf. "Oh." I hadn't felt it before, didn't even know I'd been struck. But now that the adrenaline was wearing off, it stung. "Ouch."

"Don't fear, targana. I will tend you." He pulled me impossibly closer. "The cuts are not deep. You will be well."

I grinned, despite all that had happened. "Well, at least you're talking more."

His answering snort belied that notion.

"No, you can't fool me." My smile widened. "I can see that you have real chatterbox potential, probably once you land on a subject you like. You just haven't gotten going yet, am I right?"

He didn't respond as we approached the ship. But his lips quirked. When he spotted the doorway that subtle grin vanished. He stared down at me. His brows pinched together. "What did you do?"

I tucked a piece of hair behind my ear and rubbed my neck. "Umm…about that."

Brok shook his head and turned with me in tow to study the panel. His forehead scrunched in a manner that was startling human. "How did you do this?"

"I mean, your technology is different, definitely more advanced." I leaned forward and reached into the panel, still held in Brok's arms. I loosened the cap on the green tubing with my fingers. The white one proved more of a problem. *How do I get that pinch loose?* I glanced around the compartment. "But it's not that unusual. Got any suction tools?"

His gaze dropped to my mouth.

"Ah, not what I meant." The heat in his eyes burned like an inferno. My damn cheeks flushed again in response. I'd deal with my traitorous body later. For now, we needed to gain control over the door. "I need a device that works like a vacuum. Preferably something handheld."

Brok hummed a response. "Wait here." He set me gently on the floor, but before he rose to his full height, he claimed my attention. "Do not move from this spot."

I had the startling inclination to say, *Yes, Sir.* And not in the chain of command sense. But for an entirely different reason that I was not prepared to look at too closely. I kept the instinct under wraps, but it was a close thing. I simply nodded.

He held my gaze a moment longer as if either not satisfied at my answer or not trusting me to comply. Maybe both. I didn't blame him. I wasn't exactly the obeying type. *Right?* I crossed my arms over my chest. My t-shirt rubbed against my hardened nipples. *Nope. Not at all.*

I huffed. "Go." Waving at him from my spot on the floor, I conceded. "I won't go anywhere."

Brok stared for one more heartbeat before heading out of sight.

Although I hadn't gotten a chance to explore yet, I could tell the ship's general layout. The side door, where I currently sat, was attached to the front cabin. That housed the pilot and passenger seats, the control panel, and the huge viewer. Beyond that area was a hallway leading to the back of the ship and a set of stairs to the lower compartment. Based on the ship's size, I imagined it had at least a few sleeping quarters, a food storage and eating space, an engineering room, and whatever other areas the Rhonar deemed a necessity. Given Brok's muscles, I was betting on a gym.

My toes twitched as I itched to search the ship and see if I was right. The minor movement drew sensation into my calf. I hissed. "Damn, that stings."

"We'll see to that first." Brok had returned with a white square box in one hand and an odd object in the other. He knelt next to my leg and passed me the object while he carefully rolled up the bottom of my coveralls.

"What is this?" I turned it over and rested it in my palm. It had an angled circular top and a long cylindrical bottom.

He dabbed a thick paste along my calf. It sent a blessed cooling sensation up my leg, taking away the sting. He placed a rectangular patch over it that adhered to my skin. Glancing up at me, I caught the faintest hint of a smile. "It's your sucking tool."

I blinked. "Did you just make a joke?"

He turned his head to the side, but it didn't hide his rising grin. "Perhaps."

"Oh my god. You did!" I patted his arm with my free hand. "Nice one."

His stare lingered on the place where I touched him, and my body heated under that intense look. I started to pull back, but he struck lightning quick and circled my wrist. He didn't hurt me, but his grip was firm, keeping my hand in place. "I enjoy your touch, targana."

I gulped. *Yeah, same.* Moving as much as his hold would allow, I stroked his forearm. It was smooth as the hull of a starship. Not a hair to be found. He loosened his grip as I walked my fingers up his arm. The strange tattoos began a quarter of the distance from his elbow and ran all the way to his shoulder. I let my index finger graze the edge of one intriguing symbol. It felt like a flexible metal under my touch, similar to the texture of his armor.

He stood so still at my perusal. But it was the stillness of a predator—one lying in wait before the strike.

I stopped my exploration and lifted my head. The hunger in his eyes stole my breath. With infinite slowness he took the tool from my occupied hand and set it to the side. Then he brought my palms together and clasped both wrists in one of his large hands—a gentle but unbreakable grip. Dragging my arms above my head, he held them firm, then used his free hand to wrap around my waist and pull me to his chest.

Fire coursed through my blood. The act of being held immobile against his hard body, my hands bound by his grip, touched places inside me I wasn't quite ready to examine. But my body had no reservations.

His lips grazed my ear as he said, "I'm going to claim that smart mouth of yours."

*Fuck.* I moaned. Brok might not have been much of a talker, but damn he nailed the dirty talk. My answering wetness to his words proved it.

His eyes met mine, forcing me to hold his gaze. The sensations that ran through me as the seconds ticked by were like electric shocks. A tiny centimeter at a time, he moved closer, until his breath was hot on my cheek. Just when I swore my heart was about to jump from my chest, he growled and pressed his mouth to mine—hard.

Brok might control his strength, the proof of such was evident in the way he held my arms above me without harming me, but this was no gentle kiss. He swooped in, taking my mouth, owning it, claiming it as he promised.

It was wild, uninhibited. And I never wanted it to end.

*Shit. This is crazy.* My stupid brain decided to be the ultimate cock-blocker and splashed me with a dash of mental cold water. *He's an alien!* I jerked away.

Brok's eyes went from liquid heat to stone cold in an instant. He released my hands and rose before me. His body went rigid, the same hardness reflected in his gaze. And we had just started to thaw that icy exterior.

*Idiot, Sage.* I mentally admonished. When the hell had I become so close-minded? I was an engineer in space for heaven's sake. I wanted to learn about the worlds beyond the stars. I dreamed of it all my life. *And now, what? Freaking out over a kiss?* I sighed.

Yeah, maybe it was more than a kiss, but I'd wanted it. Every part of me lit up in a way I'd never experienced before—with anyone. This alien's dominating manner stroked an inner fire inside me, touched elements of my nature I'd kept hidden for too long. So, why was I so quick to snuff it out? *Just because he's an alien?*

Shame swept through me. For always being the shortest person in any situation, I'd never felt so small.

## Brok

My mate feared me. That had to be the reason she pulled away. I had smelled her arousal, the scent sweeter than yalian blooms. I craved it already. But I'd failed the first test. *Crex it all.* I resisted the urge to roar my frustration. I'd tried to be gentle. I'd restrained her arms as lightly as I could, but my nature was to dominate, to claim. I didn't have softness in me. *I am a fool.*

I stared down at her. My looming presence wasn't helping the situation, but I radiated with too many draving feelings. I had missed emotions for so long, caught in that sickening void. Yet now… Now, I had them at last, saved from my hollow destiny by my mate, my Truxoria. I turned my head away.

I was not worthy of her.

"I will go and check our situation. I'll need to see to the engines." I motioned toward the stairs. "If you would fix the door panel."

"Wait." She wrapped a hand around my calf. Her small fingers didn't even make it half way. "I can help with that. I *am* an engineer."

I didn't look at her. I couldn't. Now was not the time to indulge my guilt. She deserved apologies. But she also needed a warrior, especially stuck on this planet as we were. I had to focus on that, on getting her to safety. Even if I did not merit such a mate, I'd protect her with my life.

"Later," I said as a deterrent. I needed time to collect my thoughts and harden my desires—and my hearts. I had to resist the mating lust, or I'd be lost to it. And she could be harmed. I would not allow that. "I must assess the damage first."

"Fine." She sighed heavily. "But Brok, I'm…"

*Do not look. Do not.* I kept my gaze locked on the stairs, but it was difficult. So crexing difficult. "What is it?"

Her long exhalation twisted my guts. "Never mind."

I nodded without turning back. Heading for the engine room, I assessed as I went. The ship had held up surprisingly well given the beating it took through the wormhole and the crash landing on the planet. "Run full diagnostics."

"Affirmative." The ship's clipped words mirrored my mood.

The engines were located at the rear of the ship in the lower compartment. Encased in a specialized alloy and surrounded by energy fields, I hoped they'd stayed intact. Without them, we'd be powerless to leave the planet. Which left me with another obvious question.

"Analyze star charts and determine location," I said to the ship's computer. My thoughts were rattled. I should have done that earlier. Instead I'd charged into a battle that I hadn't needed to fight. It was unsettling. And unlike me.

I snarled at my foolishness. Although I'd often cursed the florin for his incessant feelings, I wished he had accompanied us on this unplanned journey. I could use his help in managing these foreign emotions. As inter-dimensional beings, the florin could travel almost anywhere. But if one of their kind were not near wherever the ship had crashed, they'd be unable to hear my call.

"Complete," the ship replied. "Current location zone 17G, Meta Sector."

Fire burned my throat. *Anger? Agitation?* I groaned, trying to determine the sensation. The Meta Sector was highly populated—and highly corrupt. Riddled with territorial disputes, it was home to rival gangs, crooked overseers, nefarious pirates, and all manner of space thugs looking for a place to lie low or cause trouble. The Rhonar had attempted to help the innocent inhabitants of the different planets in this sector, like my brather Xelan and I did on Craxon. It's where we'd first discovered a Terran female. That was the good news.

The bad news was the majority of the Rhonar had left the sector, such as I, in search of Earth, while others hunted for leads on the lost Terrans from the deep-space flight that had succumbed to an attack. Even if I could contact one of my brathers in this sector, zone 17G was on the outermost edge. It might not be possible to reach *any* sentient being this far out.

Although it was a risk as anyone, friend or foe, could pick up the signal, I had to make the attempt. "Initiate long-range beacon."

If the ship was able to leave orbit, then we'd need support to make it back to the Gaian Sector and Earth. And if it wasn't… *Why are you thinking of problems that haven't come to pass?* I steeled my thoughts. My stomach churned. I could harden my mind against negative thoughts, but my body would not release its tension. I knew not what to name it, only that my chest was tight and my spine poised for battle. I was overly alert, although no direct threat loomed.

"Stars, never thought I'd miss that little furball." I laughed and the sound rang odd in my ears. I pinched my lips together and rubbed my forehead. "Enough of this."

I pushed aside the strangeness of my new emotions and focused on the ship. The engine room retained its energy shielding, a gray glow around the perimeter. Yet, my hearts sank as I spied a long crack in the outer hull that narrowed to a smaller one in the fuel tank. The gauge on the controls blinked red. Even if the ship had sustained no other damage, we had a problem.

We were out of fuel.

I spent over a span checking and fixing minor issues around the ship. Luckily, nothing was as serious as the fissure in the tank. *That* was bad enough. I clenched my fists. At last, I had no more to do but return to my waiting Truxoria.

Cursing my cowardice, I trudged to the upper deck. Sage was not by the doorway, but she had fixed the mechanism. I checked it twice to ensure it opened and closed without issue. Then, I headed for the front cabin.

She wasn't there. My hearts began to beat hard and fast in my chest.

"Location of Terran female," I barked at the ship. Nothing could harm her on board, and she wouldn't go outside alone. *Would she?* I thought back to how she'd chased after me with nothing more than a simple tool to defend herself. I pictured her causing a distraction to aid me in battle. I saw the wound on her leg in my mind's eye grow and spread. *Yes, she would.*

"Terran female is located in crew quarters alpha." The ship's answer silenced my fears and replaced them with another feeling altogether foreign but far more pleasurable.

My little mate was in my sleeping chamber.

I wasted no time in rounding the corner and heading for my room. My kedara, my life's blood, roared through my veins. The mating lust ignited into a blaze. I halted at the entry, scanning the interior. Beside the wall-to-wall screen, which currently projected a starry night, laid a bed large enough to fit a Rhonar male. The four metal posts were bolted to the floor. The cushioned interior held black sheets and an array of pillows in varying textures. After over eight cycles enduring the horrors of planet Craxon, and far too many battles before that assignment, my vice was creature comfort. I had a hard exterior, often called a statue by my brothers, but I reveled in softness. I yearned to embrace it, to know peace and tranquility in the most tangible sense, even if I could not be soft myself—inside or out.

Not spotting her on the bed, I took a few steps inside. My desk was bare save for a luxo-cube housing the remembrance of my parents. I stared at the small object. It contained several memories, most of which came from my childhood. With my paether dying when I was still a boy, my maether had taken a new mate. It was almost unheard of among our kind. Yet, my maether desperately desired more offspring. Unfortunately, she chose the wrong male.

Porlax had no honor. From a family who stayed on the fringe of Rhonar society, they thrived by remaining in shadow. It was rumored they stole from weaker species and did not adhere to our code. When the crexing male approached my maether about mating, it was for no other reason than her status and wealth. Every Rhonar had all that they required in housing, food, and universal finances. Our laws assured it was so. But our kind also rewarded those who served our people. My paether died honorably in battle and my maether worked tirelessly in service to others. They had acquired much in their lives.

And that bastard coveted all of it.

*He deserved his fate.* I shuttered at the memories of a haunted past. Never before had I experienced such strong emotions when thinking on it. Before I entered malehood and the biological curse of the Rhonar, I had not felt as much. Even after all I'd suffered at the hands of that crexer Porlax, and everything he had done to my maether, it did not consume my senses then as it did now.

A gnawing pain clawed my insides. *Rage.* The word battered my chest. Undeniable, unshakable rage consumed me. I gripped the sides of the desk. The wood groaned in response. Breathing heavily through my nose, I fought to wrestle the alien feeling under control. Images flashed before my waking eyes: a fractured collarbone on my eighth orbit, the broken sobs of my maether and bruises upon her face, and my dearest friend, the male of my *Brather*, Xelan, standing up for me and to him.

"No," I snarled. The wood snapped under my fingers, creating gouges in the desk.

A high-pitched cry broke through the haze of anger. Then a small voice whispered, "Brok?"

*Sage.* The sounds came from the cleanser. I crossed the room to the door. It cracked open at my approach, and sparkling green eyes peeked through.

"Everything okay?" The door widened enough for me to see her lush curves wrapped in a black towel. Her hair was a halo around her face, a rich brown curling behind her ears and to her shoulders. She glanced down at herself, then back up at me. "Ah. I kinda helped myself to a shower. Do you mind?"

"Not at all." All the anger that had sparked in me died at the sight of her, a new and welcome fire replacing it. I stepped forward, causing her to retreat a pace back and allow me into the cleanser. "I could use one as well."

Heat flared in her gaze. "Oh," she said, tugging the towel tighter around her. "I'll get out of your way then."

I crossed my arms over my chest and leaned against the wall. I hoped the relaxed posture might take the edge off the lust coiling inside me and make me appear less threatening to my mate. As lightly as I could I said, "Or you could join me."

Her answering laugh was not what I expected. "Ah…as intriguing as that sounds…" A gorgeous pink hue rose to her cheeks and neck. I wanted her to drop that towel so I could see if it trailed lower. Sadly, she did not. "I had a challenge the first time with that weird slime-shower. I'd rather not repeat it."

"So it's the cleanser that's the issue?" I cocked a brow at her, daring her to say otherwise.

She ran a hand through her tousled hair. "Well, who takes a shower in glittery slime?"

"It's a natural cleaning agent." A deep chuckle broke from me. "And it dissipates quickly."

"Yeah, I'd still take water, or even a heat shower, over that," she muttered. Her feet shuffled on the absorbent carpet. The cuts on her leg had closed to leave behind dull red marks, a sign of their healing. "At least the foam thing dried me off fast. That's convenient."

"Then, why are you in a towel?" The gravel in my words could not be hidden.

The flush across her skin darkened enticingly. "Oh, my clothes are dirty, and I didn't have the willpower to put them on after getting clean." She tilted her chin up, her gaze holding mine. "I was hoping you'd have something for me to wear."

A wicked smile pulled at my lips. "I'm sure we can manage something." I pushed off the wall with my foot, surrounding her without caging her in. "After our shower."

"You are persistent." She laughed. "I'll give you that."

*You do not even yet know, my Truxoria.* I'd never give in. No matter what I had to do, I would prove my worth. Aloud I said simply, "Indeed."

"Tell you what." She laid her hand on my chest, reaching up to do so. "Get me some clothes and some food. Then, tell me what our situation is here, and maybe," she rose to her tiptoes, her face coming closer to my neck, "just maybe, I'll get back in that shower."

"With me?" I added. This female was crafty. I had no doubt that she'd claim any advantage, if I was not careful. I relished the challenge.

"Perhaps." She slid a single finger along my jaw. "Let's see how it goes."

"Fair enough, targana." I moved aside, allowing her access to the door. "We will dress, eat, and talk. And then, I will begin."

"Begin?" Her nose wriggled. "Begin what?"

I leaned over her, close enough that my face was but a breath from hers. "You shall see, tiny Terran." I had removed my armor earlier, and now, I stripped my shirt to bare my chest. She gasped, and my cock jumped. Without pause, I shucked off my boots and pushed my leathers down my legs. Her nostrils flared, and she quickly spun away.

"Wh-what are you doing?" Her palms covered her eyes.

"I told you the order of things already." A heady scent filled the air, a mating call. My mate was aroused. If it would not frighten her, I'd claim her now. But behind that spike of lust was the hint of fear and it soured my desire. I'd not have her afraid. "Clothes, food, and talk. Yet, first, I too need to cleanse."

"Ah, right." She kept her eyelids shut, but removed one hand from them to wave at me. "You go ahead then. I'll just…" Her waving hand reached out blindly. "Just um…" When she hit the wall, she crept along until her fingers grazed the door frame. "I'll wait on the bed." She squealed. "I mean in the bedroom, the ah, other room."

I struggled to hold in an amused bark. *Celestia be praised. When have I ever felt so light?* Not ever. Not that I could remember. This Terran, this sweet wonderful female, utterly delighted me. I had to temper my nature, to carve my soul into the shape she needed, to whatever she desired. I'd be her perfect match. "Yes, little female, make yourself comfortable in my bed."

"You!" She spun on her heel, eyes still shut tight, and rushed out the door. "You're a menace!"

The howl of laughter could not be contained any longer. It burst from me. My Truxoria filled me with light. Every bite of hunger, every stab of emptiness was worth it, all worth it to see this new beginning. I hadn't yet claimed her, our bond only at the tenuous start, but already I was full of my mate, the void as small and insignificant as the drop of rain to the raging storm.

"Gather your strength, Sage," I said under the safety of the cleanser where she'd not hear. "You will need it, for I intend to make you mine."

Despite our circumstances, trapped on a distant planet with no clear path home, I would cherish this time. Every beat with my mate was precious. Each step closer to her a moment to be savored. For when she submitted at last, it would be all the sweeter, and our bond as unbreakable as the fabric of the universe.

"This I vow to you, my Truxoria. Our most sacred vow." I'd not say it so she could hear, not yet. My Terran mate was not ready, but I'd speak it to the sacred divine. I placed my palm on the cleanser's dark tiles, picturing my beautiful targana in my mind, and spoke the words of my people, the promise older than time. "We are One."

# 7

## Sage

I paced the floor, my towel in an iron grip. "Okay, Sage. Breathe. Think." The sleek silver floor under my feet matched the outer ring of Brok's eyes. I cursed my weakness. *So what if you're attracted to him? It's not a big deal.* I shivered, even though a pink holo-fire radiated heat from a beautifully crafted stone fireplace. I walked over to it and stared into the flames.

"Is the problem that he's an alien?" I asked into the fire as I watched the light glint off the glass cover, a bright fuchsia glow. I'd asked the question a dozen times. But I knew the answer. The *real* answer. It wasn't the issue.

The Rhonar for all their differences were humanoid. Sure they were bigger than most humans with interesting abilities, tougher skin, and wicked symbols on their arms. Well, at least, Brok had all those qualities, but I assumed others of his kind did too. And with our genetic compatibility, it was clear we'd be able to…

I glanced over my shoulder at the bed. My clit throbbed from my imaginings of all Brok and I could do between those sheets…or atop the bare desk…or in front of the fireplace. I sucked on my bottom lip. *Yeah, no problem there.*

"So?" I sighed and pulled over the desk chair, plopping onto its soft cushion. Head in my hand, elbow propped on my knee, I contemplated. The truth didn't appear in the pink flickering light, but it echoed in my heart. "He's quiet, stoic even." I grinned thinking about the chinks I'd seen in that tough exterior. His humor would be dry, sarcastic, and his smile? *Devastating.* I liked that, all of it. The problem was the rest. "He's dominant, alpha."

And there it was. I was hooked on that type. I didn't want to be. I had fought hard against my…urges. After a horrible experience in college with a complete alpha a-hole, I had lost the desire to explore that side of myself. The bastard had made me feel…used. It hadn't help that he'd targeted my deepest insecurities and laid them bare like weapons to be wielded against me. So, afterward, I avoided all men who gave off the tiniest whiff of domineering behavior.

Brok didn't simply give off the scent, he exuded the alpha aura from his every pore. I had no doubt that anyone human, animal, or alien that stood in his presence would sense the same. And I didn't know him, not really. We hadn't even spent a day together.

"Well, I don't *think* it's been that long." I rose and headed to the screen that took up an entire wall beside the bed.

When I'd first finished fixing the door panel, I'd waited a bit for Brok to return. After he stayed away longer than my curiosity could take, I'd begun my exploration of the ship. I'd found the food prep area, storage compartments, Spartan sleeping quarters, and a room that was entirely empty except for strips on the floor and walls. It had sparked my engineering inquisitiveness, and I'd searched to uncover its use. Yet, as I'd reached a hand toward what appeared to be a control panel, I'd caught a hint of my body odor, and ugh. I'd spun on my heel and into the hall. I'd planned on going to one of the empty crew quarters, but a pink light from the bottom of a door at the far side caught my eye. I'd placed my hand to the room's panel and surprise, surprise, it opened. The first sight that had captured my attention was this screen.

Standing in front of it now, I placed a tentative hand to the surface. I'd discovered that touch changed the projected image. It switched to swirls of gold and red smoke. I let them dance before my eyes for a heartbeat as my mind relaxed.

Feeling a tad vulnerable after working through my feelings, I decided to search for something to wear. I hadn't noticed a chest of drawers or a closet, but his clothing had to be stored somewhere. I trekked to the opposite wall and spied along it. Gripping the towel in one hand, I used my free hand to search the bottom to the top; well, as high as I could reach anyway—which wasn't very much. Stretching a bit more on the balls of my feet, I gained an extra inch, but it did no good. I simply could not cover much of the wall.

"Looking for something?" The deep bass had me spinning fast. Brok stood in the bathroom doorway clad in only a pair of leathers. His chest and feet were bare.

"I…ah." I remembered how to speak. I did. The right words, however, were alluding me. I opted for a simple response. "Clothes?"

His one-sided smirk softened his features. With that sharp jaw and those penetrating eyes, he appeared impassive most often, but his smiles, *damn*. He pushed off the wall and crossed to where I stood.

"You were on the right path." He took hold of my hand and placed it over his. Then, he moved our joined hands a meter to the right and slightly down. A yellow light traveled around his fingers and palm, then it disappeared and a storage unit filled with clothes emerged from the wall. He let our hands drop.

"That's convenient." I eyed the wall, wanting nothing more than to tear it apart and discover how it worked.

"Yes. I placed your clothes in a cleanser bin. They'll be ready soon." He snagged a shirt and held it out to me. "For now, you can wear this."

The shirt would fit me more like a baggy dress, but it was better than staying in a towel. I took it with a nod, waiting.

He cocked his head to the side as if in question, before turning around. "I apologize, if I made you uncomfortable earlier."

"It's…" Slipping the shirt over my head, I straightened and tapped his shoulder. "Look. I meant to say this before. I don't want you to think it's because you're an alien that I stopped our, um, kiss."

His snort said he didn't quite believe me. Facing back to me, those silver-rimmed eyes narrowed. "I do not think that."

"Oh, ah, good." I held the bunched towel between my hands. I didn't want to drop it on the floor, but more so, I needed to occupy them somehow.

"Sage," he spoke my name as if in reverence. "I understand why you pulled away. And I apologize for my behavior." He bowed his head toward me. "It has been long since I…" His gaze wandered the room as if searching for the words.

"Since you?" I prompted.

"It's not important." He scrubbed a hand over the side of his neck. "It is clear we're attracted to one another, but I do not like the fear in your eyes."

"I'm not afraid," I said on auto-pilot. He knew. Somehow this alien warrior knew, or maybe sensed my inner turmoil.

"Yes, you are." A clear scent wafted from him like the spice of a pine tree. I didn't know if it was from the shower, a cologne, or his natural fragrance, but it sent my heart beating faster. "I am a warrior, targana. I have been so for longer than I can remember." His gaze took on a haunted look, one far away, before they returned to the present. "I haven't known much gentleness."

I reached for his hand. It was true. Lingering doubts gripped me, but the pain beneath his words touched a piece of my soul. The wounded part. He carried burdens too. "I understand."

"You don't yet." He squeezed lightly where our fingers met and used his free hand to tuck pieces of hair behind my ear. "You will in time. But know this," he leaned down, so our eyes were an equal height, "I will never harm you."

I sucked in a rough breath. I wanted that to be true. Stuck on this planet with each other, hardly knowing anything about one another, well, it didn't foster immediate trust, but if we each bent a little. "Okay."

"Okay?" he asked.

"Yes." I tightened my hold on his palm. "I'll choose to take you at your word. But if you break my trust——"

"Never," he breathed. "I give you my vow."

"Then, let's start over." I picked up our hands and shook our joined palms up and down. "I'm Sage."

His eyes tracked the movement as if trying to understand. "Brokdar." He did a shake of his own, then released my hand. "But Brok will do."

"It's nice to officially meet you, Brok." I shot him a dark grin as my trademark cynicism rose to the surface. "Now, how in the hell are we getting off this planet?"

THE NEXT MORNING WE SET OUT EARLY, AND THE awkwardness between us had lessened. Though not entirely gone, the light of day helped to dissipate the majority. After agreeing to slam the brakes on our mutual lust, or at least to slow it down, Brok had filled me in about our fuel situation.

"The ship has located a replacement source about twenty stargans from here." He'd pointed to the purple mountain range in the distance. "We can collect it and fix the fuel tank."

I'd hoped that a "stargan" was the relative equivalent of a mile, but even so, it would take a day or two to hike to the source. Back in my coveralls and boots, with my astro-wrench in its thigh holster and a pack slung on my back, I was as prepared as I could be for a trek over alien terrain. We'd each filled up a pack with water containers, protein bars, and trail mix—at least the Rhonar equivalent of those items. Brok had also given me a sheathed knife to stash in my coveralls' pocket.

"Ready to go?" Brok stood on the shoreline dressed in the same style of outfit as yesterday: leathers, boots, and chest armor. His battle ax now rested between his back and the pack he carried. I'd offered to haul his share of the food and water, so he could easily grab for his weapon. But that was met with a decisive grunt.

The dinozard, which had been unconscious when we last left it, was no where in sight.

"Yeah," I said, scanning the tree line. Tracks led in the opposite direction from our path today. I took little comfort in that. "Any idea what we might run into out here?" I waved at the forested area and the purple mountains beyond.

He shrugged. "Whatever fate decides."

"Not helping," I muttered, but met him on the shore. "Let's get going before I change my mind."

"We have no choice, targana." His face which was so hard as he stared at the road ahead, softened when he turned to me. "But we will make it."

A lick of doubt wanted to counter his statement, but I let his confidence bolster my courage. My go-to pessimism would not help matters. So, I nodded at him instead. "Right."

I walked three paces forward before a firm grip clamped around my shoulder. "Stay close."

The usual me would have balked at that, but the seriousness of our situation coiled around us and sank into my bones. "Okay."

We walked that way in comfortable silence. Neither of us getting too far ahead or behind the other. Brok must have slowed his pace considerably to accommodate my shorter legs, but he didn't say a word about it. Nor did I feel like a burden, instead it was almost like we were, well, a team. It was nice, even if everything around us appeared made to kill us.

The forest had more than gray trees with crimson leaves. Although those were beautiful in a fantasy holo-vid sort of way, the ground was squishy and plagued by sprawling roots. Not quite mud, but definitely not dirt, it had the consistency of a thick gelatin. Hiking on it was bad enough, but add in the tangles that stuck from every direction and it was a nightmare.

"How far do you think we've gone?" I tried, I did, to keep the whine from my voice. Yet, my feet had gone from aching to blister-forming. I enjoyed hiking. Heck, even rock-climbing with my baby sister was *mostly* fun, whenever she dragged me. But this? No, thank you. Every time my foot landed on the gelatinous ground, it sunk in that much deeper. By what felt like the hundredth hour, my boots were sinking to the ankle.

Brok glanced through the treetops. The planet's sun shone an orange hue as it found the nooks and crannies of the spaces between the leaves. "Not far enough."

I groaned. "Can we at least rest?"

His answering grunt revealed what he thought about that idea.

"Fine." I huffed past him, each step sending a throb to my toes. "You know just because you're some big, tough alien warrior, doesn't mean we can't take a breather."

"Sage." His warning tone grated my nerves.

I waved a hand over my shoulder without looking back. "No, don't bother. If you want to keep going, then let's—"

"Sage!" The thread of fear in Brok's shout shook me to the core.

I had no sooner froze when the ground beneath me opened up. I was staring into a massive hole that shone with a hazy light. "What the—" I didn't finish the thought as a brilliant white flashed over me and I sailed downward. A swishing noise assailed my ears, and then I was floating, but fast. Like a wind-tunnel had sucked me up, I went sailing skyward. My stomach churned. No sooner had I gotten used to the motion when I was tipped like an old-fashioned carnival ride and fell again.

"What's happening?" I cried. The light was too bright for me to see much, and the motion too fast to track, but I caught glimpses of the forest's crimson leaves and the black gelatinous dirt.

Through the terrifying ordeal, I was dimly aware of Brok's calls. "Hold on!"

*To what?* I fell and floated, fell and floated. Although I didn't think I'd left the forest, based on the snippets I did see, I couldn't reach for anything. It was like being caught in a tornado that tipped end over end. One minute it spun up, the next it spiraled down.

I held a hand over my mouth. We'd had breakfast on the ship that morning that consisted of an oatmeal-like substance, except it was the color of ripe blueberries. I did not want to see what that looked like coming up.

"Here." Brok's voice broke through the haze of nausea. "Catch!"

A thick root with black stripes all over its gray base flashed inches from my face. Instinctively, I grabbed it and tucked it to my chest. My legs wrapped around the lower part, and with a yank that threatened to bring up that blue mush in my belly, I broke free of the weird tunnel. The root dropped from my grip as I fell. "Oof."

The breath knocked out of me. I closed my eyelids tight, the blinding white light of the loop temporarily blinding me. Reaching a free hand toward the ground, it felt much harder than before. Blinking my eyes open, I saw why. Brok was sprawled beneath me, his large body breaking my fall.

"Brok?" I whispered, my body trembling after that encounter in the carnival ride from hell.

He lifted his head and captured my gaze. "Are you all right?"

My breasts were squished against his chest armor while my legs were tucked up on either side of his hips. My face was even with his collarbone. The churning in my stomach had subsided, butterflies having taken the place of nausea. This close to him that delicious pine scent invaded my senses. I had the unstoppable craving to lick the exposed bronze skin at his collarbone that snuck from the top of his armor.

"Ah." I sat up abruptly, trying to shake the urge. "Yeah, I'm okay."

The new position meant I was straddling his waist. With my words of assurance that I was fine, something sparked in his gaze. Something that was matched by the fluttering in my belly and the beating of my heart. "Sage," he growled my name. "Rise or come back down." His large, warm palm grasped my thigh. "But decide quickly, for if you do not," he pushed me backward, until my core met his cock—his clearly aroused and very large cock, "I will take the heat in your eyes and the sweet scent of your cunt as answer."

*Oh fuck.* I was in so much trouble.

# 8

# Brok

THE SCENT OF MY TRUXORIA'S DESIRE FIRED MY BLOOD, and all that heat rushed straight to my cock. She bit her lip as if torn on the decision. I waited, palming her hips. I'd either help her rise or grind down on me. The ache of that moment was sharp, but exquisite, as if I waited on a knife's edge. I hungered for her answer, but I held still, so still as not to scare her into flight.

A beat later, she leaned over me, her rich hair falling onto my chest. "This is crazy," she said, her breath on my neck. "But I want you." Her palms skimmed my armor. "So bad."

That was all I needed to hear. I surged forward, wrapping my arms around her back and claiming her mouth. She did not remain idle. Her fingers sought my hair and tore at the tie binding it at the nape of my neck. When it was loose, she dove in. Her blunt nails scraped my scalp. I explored her, sought her tongue and dueled with it. Her scent rose higher, driving the mating lust to new heights.

Moaning her pleasure, she ground her pussy against me. Although covered by too much clothing, her heat penetrated through my leathers. I tugged at her hair, pulling her head back and angling it to bare her neck. I licked along the sensitive skin, working a path to her collarbone. Her shirt, and the attire she called "coveralls", blocked my journey.

"Remove these." I fingered the straps of the coveralls. Moving her head so her eyes locked with mine, I added, "And your shirt."

Sage gasped, but her scent intensified. Blinking once, she said, "Okay."

I released her only long enough to allow her to comply. Her hands trembled slightly as she undid the straps, and then, they lingered on the hem of her shirt. My mate was not one for hesitation. She had fixed a machine with nothing more than a primitive tool. She dove into space wearing minimal protective gear. She caused a distraction against a beast many times her size, and then, knocked the same creature unconscious. Did she fear me still?

I let go of her hair and placed a halting hand atop hers. "If you are not ready, targana. We will stop."

She blew stray strands of hair from her face. "It's not that. I am just, well…"

"Look at me, Sage." I tilted her chin to me. "You may tell me."

"I know it's silly." Her heart beat loud. She had but one, yet it was strong enough for me to hear. "I'm confident in most things, but not," she waved a hand between us, "this."

"You refer to mating?" I struggled to understand her meaning.

"Sort of." Clipping her straps back in place, she rose to her feet and stretched her arm as if to help me up. "Maybe we better cool this for now. Just walk and talk." Her face angled toward the treetops. "It's getting late in the day anyway."

I nodded, taking her offered hand. To do otherwise would give insult to the aid she freely gave, but I put no weight on her as I stood. "You're right, targana. We have lingered here too long." The forest had lost considerable light since we'd first trekked inside. I had allowed my desires to put my mate in danger, and that would not do. "We will continue on and find shelter for the night."

"Agreed." She slanted her head. "But what does that word mean?" Her nose scrunched, giving her an adorable expression. She pronounced each syllable of my native tongue with care. "Tar-ga-na?"

I saw now the error in my approach. We had spoken well into the prior evening, but that was of our situation and how we would remedy it. We had yet to truly know each other, to learn of one another. As we were destined mates, desire flared between us with ease. I had mistaken this for the bond. But I would not be one with my Truxoria, nor feel her warming light filling the last remnants of the void inside me, until I had claimed her heart as fully as I intended to possess her body.

"Targana," I said, thinking on the best words in her language. With our respective translators, we understood each other, but some phrases that had no direct correlation needed assistance. "It is a term we Rhonar use to describe that which is small and sweet. It's often used for desserts." My lips tugged up at the corners. "I'm quite partial to such confections."

Her laughter burst forth. "You have a sweet tooth!"

"A sweet tooth?" I clucked my tongue along my teeth, checking each in turn. None tasted as she said. "My teeth are not so."

She answered with a wide grin. "No, it means you're a lover of desserts."

"Ah." I gave her a pointed stare. "Yes, this is true."

The pinkish hue, I had already come to love, rose to her cheeks. "That's good to know."

"When we are back in Earth's space, I shall make you my favorite dessert. You will try it." I leaned closer, allowing her to see the hunger in my eyes. "Then, I'll eat it off you."

The enticing pink brightened. She lowered her voice to a whisper but did not feign from my demand. "I might be okay with that."

"Good." I nodded and straightened to my full height. "That alone is motivation for us to succeed."

As we turned to endure the forest once more, I heard my mate humming a strange tune. I didn't know her Terran music, but it was bouncy and upbeat. I savored her joy, even as our journey delved into the unknown. From the glimpses she'd shared about her past, I determined she had not always known happiness. And it seemed her fear was not of me, but of males—or certain males. That thought soured my mood. No one would harm my mate again. I'd make sure of it.

Yet, how was I to earn her trust? For that I desired as much as her body. She was my mate, my Truxoria, my all, and I needed to prove my worth. If she were a Rhonar female, she'd recognize the mating lust, know it was the call of the sacred bond between us. But, as a Terran female, the idea of such a thing would be foreign, alien.

*Drav it all. How do I make her see?* The confusion of it ate at me. The craving for her grew stronger, a hunger that had to be sated. If I claimed her without winning her heart, would she still be mine? *No, I can't risk that.*

Memories of my maether after the death of my paether rolled through my mind, unwelcome as storm clouds.

She'd been a shell of her former self, the bond between them forged strong and true. But her desperation led her into the hands of that bastard. "You're as worthless as your sire," Paxon had spit the words at me, toxic as acid rain. "You will never be of value. The so-called warriors of our race? I think not." His fists hammered on my arms and back. I'd shielded my head and torso by curling into a tight ball. "You'll be lucky if you reach malehood, and if you do, then you'll know true pain." His eyes darkened to the blackest night. "This is but a taste, a pale shadow. Killing you now would be a mercy."

My maether had entered the domicile to find me bloodied and bruised, Paxon delivering blow after blow. She'd screamed, and the sound haunted my dreams. He'd turned on her in an instant, and it was then, only then, I'd had the will to fight back.

But I was young, small. My warrior training had begun, but the bulk I'd gain in the change to malehood was still orbits away. I didn't stand a chance. It did not matter. I fought.

I lost.

Yet the sounds of my maether's screams had brought Xelan, my friend who had come to retrieve me for our daily training session, into the home. He had a wooden sword between his shoulder blades, one of the weapons we used in combat practice. Wordlessly, he'd crept through the front door. As Paxon had his back to the entryway, he did not see Xelan approach. With the advantage of surprise, Xelan struck at the sensitive joint between the base of the skull and neck.

Paxon dropped to the floor.

It was on that day I swore my loyalty to Xelan, and he became of my *Brather*. The vow of which Rhonar choose their family, their kin, not by blood, but by choice. It was he who found the Terran female on Craxon, an omen of our good fortune as she was his Truxoria. He had saved the Rhonar with that discovery, and now with my mate so close, I could finally understand all that he had given to our kind. Yet, for me, he had given much more. He had saved my life and that of my maether, and Paxon was cast out of our society. I owed him many times over—a debt I'd never be able to repay.

The cost of such obligation didn't sway me from my duty. I'd gladly give my life for his, or any of my brathers. Yet, would that willingness alone deem me worthy of my mate? I had failed. Xelan had been as young as I. But he had succeeded where I had not. I fought from that time onward to become the finest warrior, to surpass all others, to protect our people.

It mattered not.

The Versaken, our greatest enemy, launched their biological weapon meant to block us from finding our mates. Instead it killed most of our females—my maether included. And so I had failed her a second time.

*I will not fail you, my Truxoria.* Sage walked a few paces in front of me, her rich hair swinging behind her. She'd bound it high on her head with a tie, the majority of it spilling from that point.

In my hearts I knew I had not earned her. I was unworthy. And the spirits of my past haunted my thoughts as if to remind me of that stark truth. A cloud of darkness formed in my chest, all too like the void that had sucked me in for so long. Yet, this swirling mass was full to the brim with emotions, dark emotions, too turbulent to name.

I watched her as sharply as any wild predator, part of me worrying my hearts' most fervent desires would never come to pass. And the other part, the darker part, fearing that they would.

## SAGE

As we hiked on and the orange light permeating the trees faded to an amber hue, Brok stayed silent. Well, more so than what I'd grown accustom to in the short while I'd known him. He walked behind me, watching my back with an odd expression on his face every time I glanced over my shoulder. He appeared pensive, his brows shifting and jaw clenching. I wanted to ask him about it, even mouthed "a coin for your thoughts" but no sound came.

*Maybe he's regretting we stopped when we did.* I absently tugged at my ponytail and pushed at flyaway strands. My lips pressed together, and I sucked in air through my nose. *Or maybe he doesn't want you.*

That voice of doubt was too loud in my head. I'd spent years silencing it, or at least ignoring it. And it was a ridiculous thought because Brok's desire had been obvious. Yet, here I was, going down the rabbit hole of insecurity. *Too fat, too short, too loud, too negative, too much.* I'd heard it from girls in high school, but I'd mostly said it to myself. And then… *You want to be a submissive, then you do everything I say. You don't get a choice.*

Oh no. I spun abruptly and headed off the path.

Brok's voice followed behind. "Sage, where are you going?"

"Pee break," I huffed, not wanting to break down in front of the alpha alien warrior.

He stopped, but called louder, "Do not go far. Stay in sight."

"I'm not having you watch me pee!" My eyes already stung with unshed tears. Damn this weakness.

"I will *not* watch." His exasperation was evident in his tone. "But remain in view."

"Fine." I didn't have time to argue. I ducked behind a tree, ensuring that he could catch a glimpse of me. Then, I let the anxiety flow. It gripped me hard, squeezing my chest and forcing the oxygen from my lungs. *You're such a pig. Who would want to be with you?* I counted the leaves on the nearest branch, noting their color and shape, then I did it with the next, and the next. I repeated the grounding technique, until my heartbeat settled. The shadows of that bastard's voice still echoed in my ears, but I would not give in. I hadn't consented to his verbal abuse, and I certainly hadn't wanted to be treated like I was used gum under his shoe. "It wasn't my fault."

"Sage?" Brok's giant form came into view, and I took a step back. His eyes widened. "Do not be afraid."

I fought, hell, I fought it so hard, but the tears flowed. I swiped at my eyes, furious with the moisture gathered there. "I'm not scared. I'm pissed!"

He looked around, a touch of helplessness in his gaze. He sniffed the air. "Were you unable to relieve yourself?"

"What?" Here I stood having an emotional breakdown, and he was… "Oh. Oh my god." The tears stopped, and a rolling chuckle broke free. "Are you checking if I peed?"

His brows rose to his hairline. "You made strange sounds, and took a long time. I thought you were having," he waved toward my crotch, "trouble."

I wheezed. A straight up lungs compressing, nose snotting, eyes watering, belly laugh seized me. I cackled so hard, my spine cracked. So hard my chest ached. "I-I wasn't…" I clutched my sides but the laughing fit continued. "N-not…" Sucking in big gulps of air, bent over with hands on my knees, I tried to get my amusement under control. But, damn, given the circumstances and the emotional one-eighty, I was reeling. "H-having tr-trouble."

"That's good." He scanned me head to toe as if trying to assess the issue.

When I could cease laughing, I rose and wiped the (happy this time) tears from my eyes. "I'm okay, Brok. Just having a moment."

He took a step closer, measuring my reaction. "I understand." His hand landed lightly on my shoulder and gave a gentle squeeze. "I too am burdened by," he tapped a free finger to his temple, "this."

A shuddering breath ceased me. I nodded.

With infinite care he wrapped his arms around me, pulling me against his chest. I hugged him back. "You may share your burdens with me, targana. I will listen." He leaned away so I could see his face. "I'm good at that, no?"

I snickered. "Well, you're silent enough."

He chuckled. "That is a yes, then."

"Yeah," I held tight to the strength of him, my cheek against his armor, "I suppose it is."

# 9

## Sage

Dusk settled around us, but we hadn't yet found a place to shelter for the night. On the plus side, the forest floor opened, allowing the planet's setting sun to cast its light on the ground. Our progress through the gray and crimson trees was such that the purple mountain range laid much closer than it had been when we started.

"Do you think we'll make it there tomorrow?" I asked, squinting to determine the distance to our new fuel source.

Brok retrieved the positioning device he'd stashed inside of his chest armor. Flipping it over in his palm, he glanced at it, then to me. "It's not much further." He tucked it away. "After we've slept the night, we should arrive by midday."

"Good." I sighed and fanned my face. Although the climate on this distant world was tepid, I'd grown accustomed to the moonbase's artificial controls, which kept a steady chill in the air. My neck sweat had the strands of hair from my ponytail sticking to my skin.

"Yes, but we must find a place to rest before that star skims below the horizon." He pointed at the sun that sank dangerously low in the sky.

"Okay, you go that way." I waved at the right side of the forest opening. "And I'll go this way." I motioned toward two hills that gradually grew in size to form the base of the wide mountain range.

His eyes narrowed. "No, targana. We should not separate."

"Oh pish." I uttered the phrase my mother loved to use when she'd had enough of my sisters and I bickering. "It's faster and more efficient to find a spot to make camp if we split up."

The soles of his booted feet sunk into the ground as he set them shoulder width apart. His arms crossed over his chest. "I do not think—"

"Nope." I silenced him with a palm out. "You do not get to pull the 'me big strong warrior, you little Earthling card' on me."

He reared back, his arms falling to his sides. "I have no idea what you—"

"Hold on, mister. I'm not done." Wagging my finger at his nose, I stepped closer. "I am *not* going to sit around while you scout, and it makes no sense for us to do it together when we can cover more ground apart. And further—"

Grasping my wagging finger, he brought it to the center of his chest. He pressed my palm there, splaying my fingers over his armor. "What I was going to say is, if you insist on separating, than take this," he handed me the positioning device, "and I will take the hills."

"Oh." My lips pursed around the word, and I blew out a breath. "Well, I do know how to rock-climb, so the hills aren't a—"

He silenced my tirade with a kiss. Our lips met, his gently coaxing mine apart. His tongue swept inside, banishing all thoughts. His hands skimmed my lower back and the top of my ass. He circled around to my hips, and slowly urged me away. "Sadly, my Truxoria, we must stop," he put more space between us, "before we're forced to sleep under open sky."

My head was spinning and my libido spiked out of control, but a tiny rational part of my mind registered that he was right. *And what did he call me?* I stared up at him. "You said a new word."

He stiffened then shook his head. "Did I?"

I eyed him suspiciously, not certain of my conviction. "We'll settle that later. For now, we need to get moving."

"Yes." Swooping back in, he circled his arm around me once more. "But be careful." He placed a kiss on my brow. "And stay where I may hear you."

Warmth spread through me. I grinned. "Okay."

Still holding me in his arms, he lingered for several heartbeats before finally releasing me. As he headed toward the hills, he kept glancing over his shoulder at me. To be fair, I did the same, reluctant to move from my spot and lose sight of him.

It was odd how quickly I'd grown attached. I wasn't the love at first sight type. With past boyfriends, it had taken me time to feel any sort of attraction, let alone something more. And that had been before J.J., aka asshole from college, had soiled my dating life. Still, I couldn't deny there was something between the big alien and me.

With effort, and a few minutes later, I got my feet moving and scouted the terrain. The forest had opened considerably with a span of at least ten yards between trees. I was hopeful we'd be able to find a sturdy overhang or a fallen tree to use as shelter. But the more I looked, the less I liked about the place. Sure it had open space, but it was damper than the denser woodlands with too many places for unfriendly eyes to watch a sleeping camper.

"This won't work." I spun around, ready to follow my trail and find Brok. That's when I spotted the most alien thing I'd seen yet...well, second to the dinozard. "What in all the galaxies?" An enormous, fiery red bush with leaves as delicate in appearance as goose feathers was home to bright yellow blooms. In a pinch, they might have passed for sunflowers, at least in color, but the shape was wrong. The petals curved inward forming perfect spheres as big as volleyballs. "So, yeah, that's weird."

I inched closer. I wasn't a botanist, preferring mechanical over biological studies, but my curiosity simmered nonetheless. I sniffed toward one of the flowers, staying over an arms length away. I didn't dare put my face too close. I smelled nothing. Reaching for a fallen stick, I tossed it at the bloom. It swayed with the impact, but otherwise had no reaction.

"Oh, come on. Are you afraid of a plant?" I took another step towards it. *Then again, it could always be a human-eating Venus flytrap.* Pinching the bridge of my nose, I warred with my indecision. Seconds ticked by. My heart pounded in my ears. "This is silly. And you don't have time for it." As if in answer, an ominous crack of thunder roared overhead. I jumped back. "Shit!"

The noise jarred my senses. I was supposed to be searching for shelter, not studying a flower. I turned away as the clouds opened and fat raindrops poured down. I skimmed the trees for shelter, but before I could choose a direction, something struck my backpack. I stumbled forward to my knees. "What the hell?" I spun on the ball of my foot, rainwater hitting my head and dripping into my eyes. "Whose there?"

Shielding my forehead to keep the rain off my face, I tried to spot what had hit me. One of the huge, yellow blooms rested near my foot in the dirt. I watched in horror as tons of long, spindly legs slipped from beneath it while a mouth appeared at the top, housing multiple sets of fangs. I yelped at the flower-spider hybrid and fell on my butt. My palms hit the dampened dirt beside my hips and sank in.

"No! Stay back." I kept my gaze glued on the freaky creature.

The flower-spider advanced. Somewhere, somehow, a shred of my survival instincts kicked in. I yanked my hands free from the dirt and grabbed my astro-wrench from its thigh strap. My other hand plucked the knife Brok had given me earlier from my coveralls. I flipped my legs to the side and managed to crouch with my weapons raised in front of me. My pulse accelerated as did the rain. It became harder to see as the droplets grew bigger.

A hiss accompanied the first attack, helping me track the creature's movement. It had jumped, its many legs propelling it in a high arch. As it descended, I rolled to the side, out of its reach. It landed with a squelching sound into the now drenched ground.

"Nasty." I grimaced as my stomach rolled. I had eaten an alien version of a protein bar as we walked earlier, but it had been awhile ago and my gut clenched on whatever was left of it.

The flower-spider regained its footing, each of its legs pulling free of the muck with a loud sucking sound. It did not help my nausea. I braced, rising to my full height. I had the advantage of size—for once—and hell, if I wasn't about to use it. The creature appeared undisturbed, its fangs turning in my direction. It had no discernible eyes, but the hairs on my arms stood on end. It felt like it was watching me.

I shouted at it, too frazzled to use caution. "Come on then. What are you waiting for?"

The creature jumped again, this time rising impossibly higher. It sailed over my head, three of its legs swiping at my face. I ducked and struck with my astro-wrench. It caught the edge of the flower-spider's rounded body, knocking it off course. It careened to the ground and flipped to its back. The long, spindly legs wiggled in the air.

"Hah," I said, spinning my astro-wrench once in victory. "Not so tough now, are you?"

A piercing wail shook the forest floor. Answering cries echoed the noise. I gulped, gripping tight to my weapons. I spun in circles to locate the source of the noise, but I couldn't see anything as the rain increased ever more. Another crash of thunder added to the cacophony. A bolt of lightning lit the woods around me, and what I saw turned my blood to ice.

"No!" I added my scream to the chaos.

The blood red bush had lost all its yellow blooms. I had but a glimpse of them through the storm's lightning strike, but it was enough to see the legs sneaking out from under each of those things. Long, spindly legs from flowering petals and fangs that glimmered in the darkness.

I shivered, but not from the rain. I backed against the trunk of the nearest tree. I was not about to let those little bastards come at me from behind. When one of them landed on my boot, I screamed again and shook my leg like a wet dog. "Get off me!"

The creatures closed ranks, near enough for me to make out their forms even in the torrential rain. I held my knife and astro-wrench at the ready, but I knew the outcome.

They were so many…too many.

I let out a choked sob and then steadied my footing. If this was the end, then I would go down fighting. I thought of my sisters, my mother, my friends, hell, even that damn fuel-converter that I never got to finish fixing, and the big bronze alien who had gotten under my skin.

"Brok," I whispered. The connection between us had sprung from no where, hard and fast, but no less real. I regretted not having the time to see where it could lead, what it could grow into given the space to do so. And that was when it hit me… *Brok said not to be out of earshot.* I was an idiot.

"Brok!" I screamed his name at the top of my lungs. *But shouldn't he have heard me before?* I didn't have time to wonder if the rain had drowned out my cries as the first set of creatures made their move.

One landed on my shoulder, clamping its legs around my upper arm, while the another aimed for my knee. I shrugged the lower one off with a solid kick, and used my knife to stab at the other. It squealed as the weapon sliced through two of its legs. The hissing admitted from the remaining horde was chilling. Having tested me, they now moved as a unit over the ground in my direction.

I struggled not to close my eyes. I didn't want to see their attack. Fighting was my only option, but damn, I'd be lying if I said I wasn't terrified. Just as I thought I'd surrender to the fear, a shadowy figure appeared in the rain. Taller than a bear, it stalked forward, growling its wrath. The flower-spiders stopped their progress as if unsure which way to turn.

Lightning struck again, and I gasped. Brok was the figure in the dark. With battle ax in hand, he stood dripping wet and rage spilling from every pore. His roar split the heavens. Faster than the storm, he swung, sending the creatures careening like old-fashioned bowling pins.

"Over here!" I shouted, waving my arms to get his attention.

The silver of his eyes gleamed as he focused on me. His heavy boots left muddy footprints in the ground. When he came within a hand span, he looked me up and down. Seemingly satisfied with what he found, he grabbed me around the waist and slung me over his shoulder.

"Hey!" I beat my fists against his back, noting absently he no longer had his pack. "Put me down. This isn't funny."

"Quiet." He growled, smacking my ass. It wasn't a hard slap, but the sound of it in the rain was a wet sloshing thud.

I yipped. "Brok!"

"Do not test me, Sage," he barked as he plowed like a predator through the downpour. Yet, his next confession tugged at my heart strings. "I am on a fine edge." It was only then I noticed how his arm shook against my thighs where he held me to him. His other hand carried his ax at his side. "I didn't hear you with the crexing storm. I didn't hear you!"

"Whoa." I went from beating his back to petting him wherever I could reach. "It's okay. I'm fine."

His shuddering breath vibrated through him and into me. "I couldn't find you. I searched all over these drav woods." Fingers tightening against my legs, he moved faster. "Your scent disappeared. Your tracks lost to the rain. I called your name, but nothing."

"I'm here, Brok." Hanging upside down on his shoulder was not the best time for a heart-to-heart, but I understood the desperation, the vulnerability in his tone. "Everything is all right."

He didn't speak for a while, and I let him ruminate, although I really, *really* wanted off his shoulder. The caveman act might be hot in romance stories, but in reality, that muscular shoulder dug in. Luckily, I didn't have long to wait. Brok delivered us to the mouth of a cave, and once inside, he set me on my feet. I was so happy to be out of the rain, I almost dropped to my knees then and there to kiss the dry floor. Then, I thought about the flower-spiders and what could be lurking on the ground and stopped.

I spun around, my wet hair spraying water everywhere. Crystal segments alighted the cave interior in a soft bluish-white glow. "Good find."

He grabbed hold of my arms and pulled me within inches of his face. His breathing had evened but that hard look remained in his eyes.

I trailed my hands up his chest, over his neck, and cupped his cheeks. "Brok, I'm okay."

A heartbeat at a time that glow in his gaze changed to something…hot.

I wanted that heat, that fire. After almost losing my life to those creepy flower-spiders, I didn't want to deny what burned between us. With his face still clutched in my hands, I planted a hard kiss on his mouth. "I need you."

# 10

# Brok

I'D ALMOST LOST MY MATE. *CREX!* THE MENTAL CURSE didn't satisfy the storm raging inside me, more turbulent than the one outside. When I first found the cave, I'd been elated to have provided proper shelter for my Truxoria.

Then, she'd disappeared.

I scoured the woods, as fast as any native creature to this accursed planet. Yet, the rain had flowed, wiping away all signs of her. The fear I had known in that moment was unlike anything I'd experienced before.

Now, Sage stood before me. My body tightened at her touch. Her lips on mine was a balm to my soul, but the doubt in my gut lingered—a living beast that ate at me. I would not give in. She was here, safe, and begging for my claim.

I'd deny her nothing.

Lifting her easily, I guided her legs to wrap around my waist. I had scouted the cave earlier, dropping my pack near the kindling I'd collected. The back of the cave broke off into smaller tunnels. I didn't have time to explore them, but a fire should keep any lurking creatures from our claimed space. With the rain outside and the oncoming night, we didn't have much choice.

"Brok," she moaned my name, and my cock hardened behind my leathers. Her shiver, however, made me pause.

"Are you cold?" It was a foolish question. Our clothes were drenched, hair sticking to our scalps, and the setting sun turning the balmy weather to a frost.

Peeking at me from underneath her lashes, she hummed her answer. A finger curled around her wet hair. "I am, but I didn't want to spoil the mood."

My grunt conveyed my thoughts. The cavern was illuminated by crystallized formations, providing ambient light but little heat. I strode with her to the bundle of kindling and gently set her on her feet. "My pack there," I pointed to the bag beside a small cluster of rocks, "has a firestarter, a blanket, and a towel. Use them to dry and spark the flames." I motioned to the interior of the cave. "I'll collect bedding materials for us."

"Roger." She straightened her fingers and held them to her forehead, then waved her hand sharply toward me.

I nodded, assuming the gesture meant she agreed. Every step I took away from her was like a physical blow. It wasn't simply the pull of the mating bond, although that was more than enough. No, I was loathe to leave her alone. Having nearly lost her, everything in me screamed to stay with her, to protect her. But I didn't want her to pass the night in discomfort.

My need to keep my mate safe warred with my desire to ensure her well-being. "Sage," I called, no more than three yaunas from her. "Hum for me."

"Hum?" she asked as she rose to her feet with a blanket in hand.

"Yes, I need to," I paused. Would she be displeased in my revealing this weaknesses? I scrubbed a roughened palm over my face. *No. My mate is understanding. She will see the need.* If I wanted the sacred bond to take root and last, then I had to bare my soul. To do less would be a dishonor to her. "I need to hear you."

A beautiful smile lit her face, making it that much harder for me to be away from her. "I get it. I'll hum my favorite song, okay?"

Spinning the blanket in her arms, she hummed. It was a melodic tune with peaks and valleys that changed the mood of it from light and airy in one beat to deep and soulful in another. I liked it. "Yes, that's good, targana."

Another grin in my direction, and then, she knelt to the kindling. I filled my lungs to the brim, let it all free, then continued on. I wouldn't go far, but my mate's humming helped ease the weight on my hearts. I searched the interior of the cavern, scanning the walls and hidden alcoves. In one such recess, I spotted a bundle of soft plumes—a creature's nest but long since abandoned. It was reminiscent of the sao-sao bird's feathers on my homeworld. Yet, instead of green fluff, these were striking blue and indigo hues. Stripping my armor, I used the flexible frame to carry the bounty.

After four trips, I collected enough material for us to use as a pallet with a blanket draped over it. Sage had started and stoked the fire to a roaring blaze. On her knees beside it, she held out her palms to its warmth. Bathed in the firelight, her coveralls soaked from the rain, she'd never looked more beautiful. My cock ached to be inside her, but a far more pressing need fueled me.

"Targana," I allowed her to hear the gravel in my tone, "remove your clothes."

Her head tilted to the side and a knowing smirk grazed her lips. "And why should I do that?"

"You're all wet." I took a towel from my pack and handed it to her. When she gripped it, I held firm. I bent to be sure my gaze captured hers. "But I would have you wetter still."

Her gasp was stolen by my tongue. Delving in her mouth without letting her catch her breath, I snaked an arm around her. With my free hand, I snagged the straps of her coveralls down her shoulders, never breaking our kiss. She moaned against my mouth when the material slid to her waist. Her nipples hardened behind her damp shirt, rubbing against my chest.

It was not enough.

Breaking our connection for but a beat, I pushed the coveralls past her hips. She shifted to drag them down her legs. Once free of them, she tugged her shirt over her head. Clad in only her undergarments, I stared at her, wanting to see her laid bare. "All of it. Off."

Waving at me, she asked, "What about you?"

I shucked off my boots and let them hit the wall. My chest was already bare, my armor the makeshift carrier for our pallet. I kept my leathers on. I had plans for her, and my cock could wait. "Now, Sage."

She rolled her eyes, but took the band of her tight breast wrapping and pulled it over her head. Hesitating at the waistband of her bottoms, she caught my gaze. "I should tell you something first."

My throat tightened. "What is it, targana?"

"Well, I…" A long shuddering breath came forth. Not liking the far away look in her eyes, I reached for her and tucked her against my chest. She snuggled close, one arm around my waist and the other in a fist between my hearts. "I've always wanted to try being," she dipped her chin, impossibly lower so her next words were whispered over my skin, "submissive."

I stopped breathing. My mate desired to be dominated. She was truly my perfect match, and perhaps, would not shy from my demanding needs. "Why do you hide your face from me?" I put a gentle hand under her chin. "There is no shame in this. I am the same."

"You want to be submissive?" Her smile shone brighter than any star.

"No," I said firmly, narrowing my eyes, but smirking to lighten my tone. "I have an innate need to——"

"Dominate?" she finished for me.

"Yes." I hissed and held her cheek against my palm. "I had little hope to find a mate at all, but even if fate granted such a female, I never imagined she'd accommodate my desires."

She kept my gaze, but her breathing grew ragged. "That's the thing. I want to. I've always had these," her lips trembled, "urges. But well, I had a bad experience before with someone I thought I could trust."

The inferno of rage ignited within me. I recognized it now, a force so strong it blazed forth whenever my mate was threatened. I didn't shy away from it. "I will kill this male."

Sage laughed at that, but my gaze held hers captive. "Oh, I believe you. But he's not important." She waved a hand in the air as if banishing an intruding spirit. "It's just that he broke my confidence and made me feel that what I wanted was, um," her slight sniff stopped my hearts from beating, "dirty. That *I* was dirty."

My grip tightened on her, and she yelped. "Forgive me, my Truxoria, but you must be avenged. I *will* kill this male."

"Let's not talk about him anymore. I just...needed you to know." She pushed down on the waistband of her undergarment. "But I'd rather concentrate on us."

My nose flared as her intoxicating scent hit me. I needed that secret flavor on my tongue. "You are beautiful."

She blushed. "Thanks. Sometimes I feel the pressure to be skinny." Placing a hand to her rounded stomach, she gave a squeeze. Soon I'd have those lush curves under me. I'd taste every inch of that creamy skin. Her fingers brushed her bare pussy mound. "For the most part though, I'm happy with my body. I like my curves, and I don't let my past dictate who I am."

"And who you are, Sage," I surged toward her, claiming her mouth, and dipping her low over my arm, "is mine." I took control of the kiss, forcing her to take all I would give. She did so with such perfection, I groaned. I placed her on the pallet, guiding her arms above her head. "Now, targana, you must stay still." I took the towel and started at the top of her head to dry her. "If you want me to stop, choose a word to say that will cease my actions." When I reached her breasts, I patted them lightly with the cloth, everywhere but her hardened rosy peaks. "What is your choice?"

She gasped, panting as the towel went round, skating the points she yearned for touch most. "I-I can say, 'mango'." Her breathing grew shallow. "It's a f-fruit I don't like."

"Mango, then." I watched her squirm as my ministrations moved to her belly. "Sage, you're moving."

"Sorry, Sir." Her eyes gleamed bright green in the firelight.

My cock jumped at her use of the honorific as my translator deciphered it. Yes, I liked that very much. But I would not be rushed. Drying her legs and feet in turn, I purposely skipped her glistening pussy. My mouth watered for a taste, but I fought the desire with an iron will. I had not been venerated as *the* stoic warrior without cause. When every inch of her was dry, I used the towel to pat my own skin, then laid it in her hands.

"You may hold this and squeeze it if the sensations become intense." I made sure she understood each word. "But you are to keep your hands where I've put them, and…" I blew on her right nipple. She jumped. "Do…" I did the same to the left. She wriggled in place. "Not…" I gave her pussy a light slap. "Move."

Her hips bucked. "I-I c-can't help it, Sir."

I gripped her ass cheeks, loving the fullness in my grasp. Angling her high, I placed a bundle of feathers underneath, then draped each leg over the side of my makeshift cushion. I sat on my heels and stared at her spread and open for me. She was gorgeous, her pussy like a blooming flower and glistening with her dew that was all for me. I licked along my teeth already imagining the taste. But first…

"If you are a good girl," I motioned to my cock still bound behind my leathers, "you may have this." I rose to my feet and circled around her side. Her eyes tracked my movements. "If not, then I'll have to punish you." I knelt again and bent over her right breast. Swiping fast at the nipple, she tensed but did not move. "Ah. That's a good girl." I smirked. "You understand?"

Her skin flushed that pinkish hue I loved. "Yes, Sir."

"Now, hold still," I said and devoured her.

## SAGE

*Hell on a stick.* I planted my feet on the cave's solid ground. My knees were bent and angled open, exposing my pussy to the elements. My hands were over my head, towel gripped tight, and bound by Brok's command alone. It was more amazing than I'd ever dreamed, and we'd only just started. I reveled in my submission, feeling truly alive, truly myself for the first time in my life.

Brok drew lazy circles around my breast while keeping eye contact. Every second I closed my lids too long or let my gaze fall away, he brushed my nipple with his callused finger. I moaned, needing the firm contact. But he kept me on edge, not allowing an ounce of relief, until he was ready to give it to me. I panted. I moaned. I begged. And I loved it. All of it.

When I thought I'd fall apart from the teasing, he clamped his lips around my nipple and sucked—hard.

I screamed.

Then, his tongue vibrated. Fucking vibrated! I wailed. He eased back a touch and used sharp flicks of that vibrating tongue to prolong the sensation. Sucking and licking in turn, until I was a sobbing mess. His eyes were black as night in the light of the fire, the silver on the rim like a band of stars. When he finished with my right breast, he asked, "Mango?"

I shook my head vigorously side to side.

That half-grin I was definitely a fan of appeared, and he moved soundlessly around my body. He paused by my head and rubbed my arms. The blood flowed through them, causing tingles. When he was satisfied with that, he crouched over my left breast. He repeated the torment he'd given all over again.

"Brok, please," I cried his name. The pressure of his vibrating tongue dancing over my skin while avoiding the spot I needed him most was too much. He didn't stop the torment. Over and over he circled, but never touched the tip. When I thought I would implode from the building tension, he sucked my breast—my entire breast, taking as much as he could into his mouth. His teeth grazed my skin. His tongue rasped along my peak as he sucked.

"Fuuuck," I groaned.

He set it free from his mouth with a loud popping sound. Then, he began the teasing flicks from his tongue on my nipple. The sensations drove me wild, my pussy clenching at emptiness and begging to be filled. I had long since disobeyed his command to remain still, but he didn't reprimand me. Stalking slowly down my body, he moved those agonizing licks to my stomach, belly button, hips, thighs, calves, and back up to my outer pussy lips. He blew on my clit, and I jumped again.

He hummed against my pussy mound. "Are you deliberately disobeying me?"

"No, Sir." I planted my ass on the ground and stretched my arms ever more overhead.

His long fingers circled my thighs. "Of course not." He captured my gaze and held me open with his big hands, his grip gentle but firm. "You're a good girl. But you may need help staying still, yes?"

"Yes, Sir!" I cried.

"Then, I'll hold you in place for me." He growled and the sound reverberated, tickling my skin. Settling on his stomach, his shoulders split me wider. His arms wrapped around my legs and his hands stayed on my inner thighs. "Yes, this is ideal."

I blinked down at him, not quite understanding what he meant. "What is, Brok?"

"This position." He shot me a wicked smile. "It's perfect for a slow…" He kissed my pussy mound. "Thorough…" He traced my outer lips with the tip of his tongue. "Feast." Slipping higher, he began the same torturous circles he had used on my breasts to circle, but never quite touch, my clit.

"Fuck me." I let my head fall back and stared at the ceiling.

"Oh no." He laughed. "We're not even close."

# 11

## Sage

I NOW UNDERSTOOD HOW SOMEONE MIGHT MIX UP heaven and hell. Brok licked me so long without relief, I'd have traded my soul to the devil for an orgasm. "Brok! I can't." I shook, and he held me through it. "Please, please."

He didn't answer with words. Taking two long, thick fingers, he plunged them inside me at the same time he sucked my clit. I went off like a rocket, so wet and ready, his entrance was a smooth glide. My pussy clamped down on his fingers as he curled them, rubbing that usually elusive spot inside me. And I swore, I knew it sounded unreal, but I fucking swore, I saw my spirit floating above my body. I circled somewhere around the cave ceiling before crashing back into my skin.

I panted like I'd run a marathon.

Brok stretched out next to me, shifting my legs over his hips and taking my arms from overhead to cradle against his chest. He coaxed me to turn onto my side and put my face in the crook of his neck. "Shh, my Truxoria." His rumbling tone was like a warm blanket around my overworked and overly sensitive body. He reached behind us, snagging a water container, and placed it in my hands. "Drink."

I tilted it to my mouth and swallowed in long gulps.

"Easy," he chided, pulling it away. He took a swig, and then put it aside.

A contented sigh fell from my lips. But even in my blissful state, curiosity rose. "You never told me what that other word meant." I leaned my head back to stare up into his eyes. "What is it, trucks-or-ee-a?"

He covered my hands and flattened one of my palms between his pecs. "Do you feel my hearts beating?"

I grinned, counting the double beats beneath his muscles. "Yes."

"And my joy, my happiness, is you." Brok kissed my forehead, before returning his gaze to my face. "You feel this too?"

I nodded. "I do."

"Everything, all of this," he tapped our joined hands, "is thanks to you. You are my Truxoria, my mate, and you've saved me from myself."

My brows drew together. "What do you mean?"

"Rhonar males do not simply need our females to procreate as so many species do." His jaw tightened, and his tone grew serious. "When we reach malehood, we lose all emotions. It's like being drained of all that you are and replaced with an insatiable hunger that can never be filled." A haunted look came over his eyes as he met my gaze, the light in them dimming. "But that is only the first phase. Each male moves through it at a different pace, but the second phase is the void, and it is worse than any torment I can imagine."

I sat up, startled by his words. "And this is natural for your kind?" I couldn't imagine the horror of being unable to escape such a fate.

"Yes." He sighed. "Our elders say it's to teach us to cherish our mates, to value them above all else." His eyes softened as he looked at me. "Now that I have known both the void, and the wonder of a mate, of you, I believe they may be right."

My mind spun. I had always loved mechanical puzzles, but suddenly, I wished I had paid more attention in my biology classes. The Rhonar might be the greatest medical mystery of all time. But now wasn't the moment to ponder it, the other thing he said was far, far more significant. "So, you think I'm your mate?"

"I don't think, Sage." He clasped my hands as if afraid I'd disappear. "I know you are."

"Because you have," I touched my tongue to the roof of my mouth contemplating the implications, "emotions again?"

"Yes. It has been many orbits since a Rhonar male claimed his fated mate with the exception of my brather Xelan, who found your Terran scientist Ava." Rising, he pulled me into his lap, his fingers playing through my hair. "But each warrior experiences the mating bond differently, from what the elders say. I sensed it even before we met, but I knew it when your presence began to fill the void inside me."

The idea of Brok and I coming together through destiny was more than a little weird to me. But my bigger worry, if I were honest, was his well-being. "And you're okay now?"

"I am, targana." He peppered my neck with sweet kisses that made me hot despite how hard he'd made me come only moments ago. Picking up his head, he added, "When we are one, all echoes of the void will fade. We will have the mating mind speak, and no one will separate us, ever." The last part he said with a firm conviction.

I shivered. "When we are..." I pieced through his words. "Oh...oh."

"Does this displease you?" His chest fell.

I thought on it before answering. "No, not exactly." I put my hands on his shoulders and squeezed. "It's just kind of a lot."

"Ah, I see." Carrying me to the pallet, he guided me to lay on my side once more. "It has been a long day, and you are tired." He swept a blanket around me. "I should not have said so much."

I giggled, not my usual belly laugh, but a tiny giggle. I was mildly horrified at the overly girly display, but it mattered little, since I felt so at ease with Brok. "See? I knew you were secretly a chatterbox."

"Yes, my mate is wise." He stirred the fire, ensuring we had enough kindling for the night.

I stretched like a contented cat, only to see the bulge in his leathers as he rose. "Oh shit!" I sprung up. "I'm so sorry. I didn't think." I motioned at his pants. "You didn't get anything in return this whole time."

His bark of laughter echoed off the cave walls. "Not get anything?" His tone was incredulous. "I tasted the most exquisite delicacy in the universe." He crouched, meeting me at eye level. "I am already desirous of another feast."

My eyes widened. "Oh no!" I held up my palm. "I cannot take that again." A snort told me he thought otherwise. But I held firm. "Brok, no."

He sighed like someone long suffering. "If you *must* rest."

I giggled again, slightly less horrified by the sound than before. "I was talking about taking care of you." I waved toward his cock.

His eyes heated, but he shook his head. "No. If we travel that road, I will claim you fully, and you need to regain your strength before that."

I pouted. "But—"

"Do not look at me that way, Sage." He leaned against the far wall at the mouth of the cave. "I'll stand guard while you sleep. If you continue to stare like that, I cannot be held responsible for your tiredness tomorrow."

"Wait, you're not going to rest too?" My concern for him doubled.

His grin was far too proud. "Rhonar need less sleep than little Terrans."

I rolled my eyes. "Fine, big bad alien warrior," I flopped onto the pallet, "do your thing. I'll just dream of your big bad cock and what I'd like to do with it."

His groan was the most satisfying sound as was his grumbling words, "Earning punishment."

I snuggled into the blankets, thinking of what delicious discipline I could earn tomorrow.

WHEN I AWOKE THE NEXT MORNING, MY BODY THROBBED and ached. But I'd slept better than I had in years. "Those feathers must be magic," I said as I stroked one of the plumes between my thumb and index finger.

Turning to find Brok already strapping on his armor, I licked my lips. "Or maybe it was just the orgasms."

Despite his instance that I needed rest, he roused me twice during the night with his head between my thighs. Not only did the Rhonar male sleep less than the silly human, apparently, he also had an insatiable appetite for...

"Does my mate need a reminder?" His words may have been in jest, it was hard to say, but his sharp eyes were all heat.

I donned my, thankfully, dry coveralls and crossed my legs while standing. "Nope. This shop is closed for service."

"Hmm." He grabbed my pack from the ground, throwing it over his shoulder beside his. "For now, I'll allow it."

Old me might have bristled at that commanding display, but after last night, well, not so much. My panties were damp with my arousal. I did, however, grip my backpack from his shoulder. "I can carry it."

"Targana, grant me this favor." He stroked a hand across my cheek. "I wish to make our trek easier on you." I opened my mouth to speak, but he held up his large hand. I couldn't help but be transfixed my those long, clever fingers. He touched my lips. "I know you are capable, strong, smart." I nodded in a *go on* gesture. "But if I can do this simple thing for you, an act that is no trouble to me, why would you deny me?"

Oh, my big bronze alien was tricky. I'd bet he had everyone fooled with that stoic as a statue act, but I saw him clearly. He had a plethora of pretty words to win people over. And every single one of them worked on me because I knew in my heart, he meant them all. "All right, Brok." I sucked on my cheek to hide my grin. "Carry my bag."

His answering smile lit up my world. Hell, he was a devastatingly handsome and oh-so-biteable alien warrior. "Thank you, my mate. I'll weigh this boon you offer against yesterday's defiance when I determine your punishment." With that, he stalked from our cave and toward the mountain paths so fast that my head was still spinning by the time I caught up.

"Hey!" I shouted as I slapped his shoulder. "That was—"

"Arousing?" He offered before I could answer.

I clamped my thighs together, cursing my stupid, horny body. "No."

He sniffed the air, then narrowed his eyes at me. "Lies will earn you more punishment, targana."

"Shit!" I crossed my arms over my chest as if that would somehow block his nose.

"Oh no, definitely not shit." He inhaled deeper. "It is the sweetest—"

I reached up and brushed my fingers over his mouth. "Do not finish that sentence."

He nipped at my thumb.

Our playful banter might have continued for longer if a mammoth creature hadn't jumped into the path in front of us. As large as an elephant, it had a hard shelled body in a burnt orange hue, six legs with three joints on each, five bulbous eyes in a square face, and two rows of razor sharp teeth.

I reached for my knife and astro-wrench. "Why does everything on this planet have damn fangs?"

Brok put a hand on my stomach and pushed me pointedly behind him. He shrugged off our backpacks with slow movements. The crab-giant watched with its huge eyes that appeared to move independently from each other.

"Creepy crab," I muttered, sliding a bit to the right and bringing my weapons to shoulder height.

Brok's growl said he wasn't happy about my joining the foray, but if this creature attacked, I wasn't letting him fight it alone. Blue light shot in an arch, Brok's shield surrounding us. His tone brokered no argument, as he shouted, "Stay inside the energy field."

Charging forward, he swung his ax as the creature reared on its hind legs and slashed with its front.

I kept pace behind him, staying within the boundaries of the shield as he asked. But if I spotted an opening, I was taking it.

Brok's ax clanged against the crab-giant's solid front legs, the ends of which were tipped with claws. The strikes were brutal, the noise piercing the stillness of the mountain pass. The creature danced around, far too agile for its size.

I watched the pair intently, searching for a weakness on the creature that I could use to help Brok.

Agonizing seconds ticked by before I spotted it. On the lower right side of its tough underbelly, a piece of its scales was missing. Using a boulder as coverage, I crept closer. I was skirting the edge of Brok's shielding, but I had to get near enough to make the shot. If I missed, then we lost the advantage.

Glancing once behind me, I was a tad worried about the drop-off. To get the angle I needed for a strike, I had to skate near to the edge of the westward cliff. *Don't look down and you'll be fine.* Easier said than done as I teetered between the boulder and the cliff's edge. Brok's brilliant blue light held fast about me, but I'd be free of its boundary line once I made my move.

"To the void with you!" Brok cursed and delivered a vicious swing at the crab-giant. It struck the creature's shell with such force it rattled the rocks around it. But the creature appeared unaffected. It spun to keep Brok in view of its bulbous eyes. With the new positions, its body was angled in the perfect spot for my attack. I just had to get a little lower to the ground, avoid its legs, and I'd be set.

*Easy.* I strapped my astro-wrench to my thigh and held tight to the knife with both hands. *Yup, easy.* I crouched as low as I could while, ironically, crab walking toward the creature. It was even more massive from this vantage point. Its triple-jointed legs were longer than me. I swallowed. If I messed this up, I wouldn't get another shot.

*Okay, just breathe.* I waited in a squat. Its front legs kicked to the side in an attempt to catch Brok, and that's when I saw it—my chance. I pushed off my heels and launched at the creature. My knife connected and stabbed into the underbelly with the missing scale.

"Yes! I cried, stumbling backward and leaving my knife where it struck.

The crab-giant howled. Its front legs curled inward as it listed to the side. I scrambled to my feet to avoid its falling form, but just as I thought I was home free, it used its hind legs to dig into the dirt and whirl toward me. The fury in its eyes was like five living flames all focused on me.

I backed away slowly with my empty hands held high. "Nice crabby. Good crabby."

The crab-giant crept toward me. Its howl turned to clicks and clacks. I kept walking backward.

"Sage!" I heard Brok's bellow, but it was too late. In my haste to escape the creature, I hadn't noticed my nearness to the cliff. My foot slipped off the edge, my arms pinwheeling at my sides. But there was nothing to catch my balance. I teetered.

And fell.

# Brok

"SAGE!" MY HEARTS LEAPT INTO MY THROAT, TERROR A palpable beat, as I watched Sage tumble over the slope of the cliff. While my soul screamed in agony, my body kicked into gear—the actions automatic from a lifetime of battle and blood. I dove for the edge, throwing out my energy shield with more force than I ever had. The blue light cascaded over the rocks.

I squinted, trying to locate her falling form. I saw nothing but empty air. *That's impossible.*

"Hey!" A shout from somewhere over the cliff rose up. "I'm okay."

I spotted her no more than ten yaunas below, but too far for my shielding to reach. I clenched my fist and pulled back the energy. She was safe for the present—her feet planted on a ledge and her body hugged to the stones. I rolled to my side, preparing to climb down to her, when the shelled beast struck. Catching me in the side, it slammed into my ribs with a strike that rattled my bones. I hissed at the pain but quickly rose to my feet. The creature had been wounded from Sage's knife; yet, it had not been beaten.

"Enough of this." Rushing the beast, I surprised it by sliding under its seeking front limbs. Although its claws were fast enough to leave marks across my armor, I used my momentum to carry me to my goal. Spying the knife Sage used to stab the soft spot, I aimed for it with my ax and struck. The blow rang true, piercing deep into the creature's belly. When it howled and staggered this time, it stayed on the ground.

I hurried to the cliff's edge once more. "Stay there," I called to my mate. "Do not move."

"Wasn't planning on it," she shouted up at me. Her feet remained on the ledge, but it was narrow, too narrow. Her hands grasped the cliff's rocks with a knuckle-whitening grip. "It's nice here. Not much room though."

I snorted. Retrieving the packs I had shrugged off earlier, I rifled through them both. *No rope.* That wouldn't stop me. But it would take longer to climb to her and back up without it. I didn't wish to linger around the downed creature as it would draw any predators to the area.

As if the universe read my thoughts and gave answer, a hulking beast, nearly double in size to the first creature, poked its shelled head over the ridge. Its eyes tracked the one unmoving on the ground, then to me.

It shrieked.

"Crex." I put the packs aside and took a firmer grip on my ax. I didn't have time for another battle while my mate was stranded below. Again the stars delivered on my thoughts. Another beast appeared beside the first, then a third on its opposite side. "Celestia, drav it all." My curses fell on deaf ears, if our sacred divine ever listened to us mortals anyway. "So be it."

"Brok!" Sage's shouts echoed through the mountains. "What's going on up there?"

I didn't have the hearts to tell her. I leaned over the cliff to yell to her. "Everything will be fine. Remain where you are, Sage."

Her grumbles were loud enough to hear even at the top. I chuckled darkly as the beasts advanced.

Readying my stance, I assessed my foes. The center creature was by far the biggest, and likely, leader of the pack. If I cut it down, the others might retreat. I scanned their forms. The two on either side of the largest looked identical to the fallen beast. All had five eyes, six limbs, and mouths of fangs with scaled underbellies and shells along their backs. The apparent leader was darker in coloring, a rusted clay hue compared to their burnt orange shades.

The leader clacked its teeth and chaos erupted.

## SAGE

I refused to stay on this rock wall and do nothing but cling to it like a spider in its web. Brok didn't tell me what was happening above, but from the clangs, clatters, and crashes, I gathered it was nothing good. "Come on, Sage," I said to bolster my courage. "This is a piece of ice cream and chocolate cake." Scanning the possible path to the top, I added, "Look at all those handholds and footholds. No problem."

My friends and family often mistook my realism for cynicism, the curse of being a Capricorn. But I liked to think I saw the world as it was, and well, okay, maybe Brok had tipped the scales a little more to the sunny side. Either way, I was getting the hell up this cliff, and then buying my baby sister anything she wanted. If it wasn't for her rock climbing obsession and dragging me along too many times to count, I'd never have stood a chance.

I sucked in a breath. "Just don't look down."

Usually, I did this with gear, lots and lots of beautiful gear. I had hated the weight and bulk of it before, but now I'd give anything for the most intricate and heavy rig I could get my hands on. *Mind over matter. Yeah, sure.*

A rumbling snarl from above, as spine-tingling as a lion's roar, set my feet in motion. One careful step at a time, I scaled the wall. I reached a hand up, grabbed a protruding rock, found a foothold below, secured my feet, and climbed. Then, I did it again, and again. Two-thirds of the way, I paused, panting for breath.

*Almost there.* I repeated that mantra, willing my body to keep going.

A rock that I needed for my next hold was three inches out of reach. I stretched my fingers, extended my arm, and…missed. My boot slipped, and I clung to the wall with only one hand and foot to stop me from plummeting. My heart pounded triple time. "No!"

I didn't survive an explosion, being sucked through a wormhole, a crash landing, and attacks from no less than three different species of alien creatures, to die from a bunch of rocks. I skid my booted sole along the rock-face, desperate to find footing beneath me. Tears sprung to my eyes, but I didn't have a free hand to swipe them away. All ten fingers clutched the lone handhold.

I steadied my breathing and willed my pulse to calm. Glancing up, I noticed something odd. Strands of a silvery substance, almost like braided silk, hung against the cliff. Inch-by-inch they were lowering toward me. I stared, wide-eyed, as one passed my right side, then another on my left. When they reached my waist, they stopped. I leaned my head back as far as I dared, trying to see what in the infinite galaxies was on the other side of those makeshift ropes.

With the planet's orange sun shining at an angle to the cliff's edge, I couldn't see anything clearly—only faceless blobs. "Brok!" I shouted, hoping that whatever was up there hadn't hurt him. I was answered with bangs and hisses. Then, one of the blobs at the top seemed to get lower to the ground. Backlit by the sun's rays, he was a dark mass, but I could hear his chittering call. My translator didn't interpret the noise, but it sounded…friendly.

"Oh, come on, Sage." I chided my foolishness. "If they wanted you dead, they wouldn't have lowered rope." I nodded at that thought. It seemed reasonable. "Unless, they want to eat you for lunch." My stomach dropped. That was a less helpful, but also reasonable idea. *What does it matter? Brok's up there alone. I have to help him.*

That decided it.

With a long, shuddering breath, I took my right hand off the rock and grabbed the rope beside me. Tugging on it to test it, I inhaled when it held firm. With one hand on the wall and the other on the rope, I looped it awkwardly around my waist, butt, and thighs. Then, I switched hands on the rock and clutched the other rope to my chest. "Okay, now or never."

I pushed from the wall and dangled from the ropes. I almost didn't believe it. I gripped the rope in my hands so hard my fingers ached. I kept my toes inches from the rocks in case I had to make a quick grasp, but I wasn't falling. The ropes began to rise with me in tow, and I let a few of the tears that had gathered flow free. I considered them rewards for not losing it completely.

When the cliff's edge came in line with the top of my ponytail, I made a firm grab for the surface. Before I could hoist my body over the side, however, tiny hands pulled me to safety. I rested on my back, shielding my eyes from the sun and trying to figure out the forms of my rescuers.

More chittering erupted around me, but weariness set into my limbs. I closed my eyes. The stress from the fall, and honestly, everything that happened before that, had settled into my muscles and bones. For that half a second, I didn't care whether these new beings were friend or foe. If they were going to eat me, then they'd have to deal with mush because that's what my body felt like. *And now, you've gone mad.*

I snickered and opened my eyes. Round faces with fuzzy pink whiskers and muzzles stared back at me. With skin the consistency of an Earth seal's, except bright purple that gave way to darker indigo patches, and antennas like an ant's, they were by far the most adorable aliens I'd seen yet. Then, an image of the dusky rose florin popped in my head. *Well, maybe tied.* I hoped they were friends because I did not want to be eaten by a creature that looked like a sea otter dipped in purple paint.

I sat up, and they stepped back. Four of them stood in a semi-circle around me. Testing my limbs, I rose with some effort. The otter-aliens came up to my chest. "So, I get to feel like the giant, huh?" All four heads tilted in unison. I smiled, and they chittered more. It sounded happy enough. I decided to take it as a good omen.

Until, I heard a roar.

Staring over their heads, I got the full impact of what was happening. Four crab-giants laid on their bellies in the mountain pass. Brok was standing atop the center beast, which was massive when compared to the other three—and that was saying something. His ax in hand, he hacked away at the outer shell while at least a dozen otter-aliens looped rope after rope around the creature's legs. It shrieked and kicked at the little guys, but the purple ones were fast. They darted in and out of the crab-giant's reach.

When at last the beast was bested, a chittering cheer rose as high as the mountaintops. Brok and I caught each other's eye. Without words, he jumped off the beast and ran toward me. At the same time, I skirted around my new friends and bolted to him. He caught me mid-run, clasping me tight to his chest and kissing me hard. I wrapped my legs around his waist, relishing in the feel of his mouth on mine. I didn't care that I was covered in dust and dirt, him in sweat and who-knew-what from the battle. I was alive. He was alive. And that's all that mattered.

"I thought you were dead." His big hands held me up, his forehead resting against mine. "When you fell, my hearts stopped."

"Me too, big guy." I smiled and nuzzled his nose. "Guess fate had other plans."

"I truly must make a trip to a Celestian temple and thank the sacred divine." He sighed as if he didn't quite enjoy the idea.

I hummed against his cheek. "I'll thank whoever you want. Whether it's your goddess or the will of the universe, we're together, and I'm thankful for it."

"As am I, targana." He kissed me again, slower this time. His lips were soft, reverent as he brushed them over mine.

We might have stayed that way for a while longer, but the chittering around us grew louder, reminding us we were not alone. "So, um," I angled my chin toward our companions, "any idea what they're saying?"

He shook his head. "No, my translator cannot decipher their noises."

"Hmm. Well, whatever it is, I'm glad it's not them deciding if we taste better cooked or raw." I scanned my gaze over the purple masses. "At least, I think it's not."

His laughter vibrated through his chest. "No, I believe you're correct."

"Let's hope so." I sighed and unwrapped my legs from his waist, sliding to the floor. "What happened after I fell?"

The black in his eyes darkened, swallowing that silver rim. "I raced to catch you and threw my energy field over the cliff." His body shuddered in remembrance. I placed a gentle hand on his chest. He continued, "But you weren't falling. You were on a ledge."

"Yeah," I muttered, trying not to shake at the memory. "I kind of fell into that bit of luck—literally."

"I am glad for it." He touched my hair, tugging a piece around his finger. "After I spotted you, I searched our packs for rope. When I did not find any, I made ready to climb down to you." Pulling me closer still, he placed his large hand at the small of my back. "That's when the beast you had struck earlier attacked again. I managed to jab in the knife that remained behind in the creature's abdomen." He glanced over my head, taking in the sight of the otter-aliens who had gotten closer as if listening to his story. "The beast fell, but three new ones took its place." He waved at the creepy creatures behind him. "And you can see how that ended."

"Phew." I blew out a breath, shifting stray hairs that had fallen in front of my eyes. "That's wild."

"Yes," he said. "Indeed. I admit I may have had difficulty with three of the beasts at once, but then these other beings appeared." The otter-aliens drew nearer still at his words. "And although, the translator fails to interpret their language, they made their intentions clear."

"The enemy of my enemy is my friend." I grinned at the cute little aliens.

"This is a wise saying." Brok slid his hand up my back and gripped the back of my neck. "But you, my

Truxoria, have much to answer for." His kiss said he would not hear argument from me. "And you are not to put yourself in danger again."

I tweaked his nose and spun from his hold. "We'll see about that."

He growled. I laughed. The otter-aliens chittered.

"Well now," I bent to smile at the nearest purple guy, "which one of you is in charge?"

Although Brok and I couldn't decipher their noises, they seemed to understand us well enough. One of them slightly taller than the rest with a plum-colored pelt and a flower crown on its head came forward. From the higher-pitched chitter, I deduced she was female, and I appreciated my new little friends even more for their matriarchy. She waved her adorable paw at me and Brok. Then, with an expression I can only describe as a watery grin, she took my hand in her paw and proceeded down the path.

I glanced over my shoulder at Brok. But he simply shrugged as if to say, "What can you do?"

And so, we followed the otter-aliens through the mountains.

I only hoped that my instincts were right, and we weren't about to become the main course in an otter-alien feast.

# 13

# Brok

THE TINY BEINGS HELD NO THREAT. ALTHOUGH fearsome in the battle against the shelled beasts, their nature did not appear to be that of warriors. After too many years of bloodshed and war, I could sense the battle instinct in others. Perhaps not so much as my brather Xelan with his ability to feel others' emotions, or my brather Torian who could read a being's soul with a simple touch. But still, I had honed my skills, and I could tell these little ones meant us no harm.

"Do you know that mountain?" I asked the one who walked by my side and pointed to the spot that housed the material we needed to refuel my ship. The alien had a darker hide than his companions and chittered less often. In truth, he reminded me of a smaller, purple version of me.

He grunted at my question.

*The universe has a sense of humor.* I eyed him to see if he avoided my question or didn't understand it. When he smirked up at me, I suspected it was the former. "You know it, then?"

A single low-pitched chitter escaped him.

"My mate and I," I waved to Sage who walked with the beings' leader a pace ahead, "we need to go there and collect supplies."

His chitter turned angry, and he stomped his hind paws on the ground.

I couldn't be sure, but I suspected he didn't like us taking from the planet. I could appreciate that. "We do not take needlessly." I tapped a fist to my chest, paying him the same respect I would any warrior. "We only need a small amount to get home."

Round eyes softening, he hummed a reply that sounded like understanding.

I pressed the advantage. "Can you take us there?"

He stopped beside me, a paw on my leg. Slapping his free paw forward, he motioned to where Sage stood with the matriarch of the pack.

"I need to talk with her then." I smiled at the pair of females, allowing my gaze to linger on my mate before turning to the male at my side. "I thank you. And I will speak with her."

Falling into a companionable silence, I reflected on the hardships I'd endured since coming to this planet. It was a common tactic of mine to replay past battles in my mind. I assessed my weaknesses and missteps, learning to correct my mistakes. Yet now, I found emotions coloring my memories. The rage at the reptilian monster staring down my mate had spurred my actions. The fight against the yellow spindly creatures in the rain was swamped by my fear for Sage's safety. The battle with the shelled beasts, and the desperate effort to finish them quickly, drove from a desire to help my Truxoria. I'd never trade her, nor my new found feelings, for the cold emptiness of the void. But I needed to learn to regulate these emotions, or my prowess as a warrior would be at risk.

Yet, even through this analysis, as I weighed my actions against my feelings, one lingering and gnawing affliction plagued me. *I am not worthy.* It was an old, constant ache, but one that persisted. The thought sat like a stone in my stomach; the idea that Celestia had given me a miracle to show me my lack. I would continue to fail the single person in all the galaxies I'd never want to harm —my dear targana. *How am I to deny this truth?* I was damned without her. As I remembered my days before Sage, the churning in my gut increased. I could not go back to that haunted half-life. But if I was destined to fail her, how did I alter such a fate?

"It would be like changing one's stars," I muttered, lost in dark thoughts.

The feel of soft fingers caressing my side brought me out of the mire. The very one I had been thinking of, my hearts' true desire, stood by my side. "You know," she said, her nose wrinkling. "You get these lines," she brushed the pad of her thumb over my forehead, "here," then down to my temple, "and here, whenever you're brooding."

I snorted. "I do not *brood.*"

"Oh no?" Her eyes widened. "Then, tell me what you were thinking about just now?"

Did I dare? I scanned the crowd of our purple friends. The sun had sunk lower in the sky as we walked for several spans. With our companions' tiny legs, I imagined it would not be much longer until we arrived wherever they were leading us. "Not here, targana." I took her hand in mine. "But soon."

The nod she gave me revealed she was appeased, for now, and she squeezed my palm. "Okay."

I saw the path clear before me. If I wanted to be an honorable male, one deserving of a mate such as mine, I had to reveal my all to her. I could not hold onto such doubts without them festering into valleys that would drive us apart. That I would not allow. Even if she saw me as unworthy after, I had to lay bare my soul and allow her to measure the weight of my worth.

My Truxoria deserved no less.

AFTER ANOTHER SPAN, THE GROUP STOPPED AT A VALLEY near the mountain that housed our needed fuel source. I was thankful to be closer to our goal, but I had no idea how the purple beings' leader would react to our request. While we didn't need their permission to collect the material, I had no desire to offend those who had given us aid.

Sage bounced on the balls of her feet as we stared over the ridge into the village below. Tiny huts scattered the landscape. An open area in the center of the space held a large bonfire pit with logs around it that must serve as seats. The leader waved for us to take a set of steps built into the mountainside that led to the valley. Rows of the purple beings stood on either side of the staircase with spears at their sides. A smile tugged at my lips in seeing the small, purple guards. I didn't discount their abilities after watching them take down the shelled beasts. But something about these creatures, who resembled our helpful florins in spirit, pulled at my hearts.

We had to gain their permission to take the fuel. It would not sit well with me any other way.

Following the leader into the village, I marveled at their ingenuity. Although I saw no discernible technology, they had managed to carve out a section of the mountain range that met their needs. The leader showed us a building packed with food and supplies, a bathhouse where she mimed washing, an empty hut where she motioned for sleeping, and then to the central bonfire area in which she bade us sit.

Sage and I sat side-by-side on the trunk of a gray log while the leader remained standing across from us. It helped to put us at eye level, or at least Sage was eye-level. I dipped my head in hopes of making the leader more comfortable, but even sitting, I was still considerably larger than her.

A high-pitched whistle from between the leader's whiskered lips brought a smaller being running to her side. The newcomer handed her a square device and quickly scurried away—although not without widening curious eyes at us. Sage wiggled her fingers at him, and the little one ran behind a building.

"Skittish, isn't he?" she said, placing her hands in her lap.

I nodded, waiting to see what the leader presented. Clicking buttons on the device, she handed it to Sage.

"For me?" Sage asked, turning the square over in her palm. The leader chittered, then raised her paw. Although it was hard to determine, I thought I understood her motions.

I leaned toward my mate. "I believe she wants you to use it." My eyes narrowed as I analyzed the leader's movements. "Possibly to fix it?" Her paws waved in the air between us as if trading... "Ah. It's a translator of some sort." I gazed at the device, then at the leader again. "I think that's what she's saying."

Sage's jaw dropped open. "How in the heck do you know that?"

I shrugged. "I've had first contact with many aliens, and not all have developed languages." The leader observed our interaction. I wrapped an arm around Sage's waist and drew her closer to my side. I suspected the purple ones knew, but I wanted to make our relationship clear. Pointing at the device, I added, "But from her motions, I believe that's some sort of primitive translator that my be tuned to their communication patterns."

"Hmm," she flipped it over in her palm, "it does look similar to Earth's twenty-first century radios." Her pink tongue poked from between her lips, and my blood fired with desire. I pointedly ignored it. Her eyes sparkled as she viewed the device like a candied treat. "Given a little time, I think I can get it working."

Seeing my mate in her element warmed by soul. I had no doubt she would succeed. In the mean time, and with the sun dipping still lower, we both could use a rest. As much as I wanted to pursue the fuel source, it would be best if we were able to better communicate with these beings first.

The leader, seemingly satisfied with our exchange, waved at us to follow her again. We headed back toward the bathhouse, and Sage moaned when the steam from inside wafted through the open door. "Oh my gosh," she cried. "I'd trade my entire tool collection for a bath."

I chuckled. "I don't think you'll have to."

With a sweep of her paw, the leader encompassed the interior of the bathhouse. In the center was a square pit filled with emerald water. It looked deep enough to rise to my waist. On either side of it, more gray logs were placed along with baskets filled with towels. They seemed to be made of a spun material. While one of them would likely not cover even half my width, I was appreciative of their presence. She handed Sage a wooden bottle, then patted her face and body, miming washing.

Sage smiled. "Thank you!" Taking the bottle in one hand, she grabbed the leader's paw with the other and patted it. "You're so kind."

The leader patted Sage's palm in a mirror gesture and chittered. With a nod, she exited the bathhouse, closing the door behind her.

My growl could not be contained. I spun toward my mate, anxious to free her from the trappings of her clothes and wash every inch of her bared skin…then, lick her clean.

"Oh no!" She yelped, dodging my hands. "That bath is a gift from the heavens, and you are not getting your hands on me until I'm covered in soap!"

"Targana," I said, stalking toward her a step at a time. "You forget you've earned punishment."

Her eyes widened and the scent of her arousal perfumed the air. "But, the bath?"

"We'll be bathing, my Truxoria." A smirk crossed my face. "And I know just how to discipline you." I took the bottle from her hand and placed it beside the bathing pit. "Now, remove these clothes." I tugged at her coveralls. "And get in the water."

She trembled on the exhalation but her scent grew stronger. "Y-yes, Sir."

My cock hardened beneath my leathers. At last it would spring free. I had to claim her soon, yet I had not laid my soul bare. *Not yet.* No, it was not time. The moment for such talk would come later. Much later. First, I had to punish my stubborn mate.

Her fingers snagged her boots, taking them off with quick movements. I did the same, longing to be free of my clothes. When she tugged off her coveralls and t-shirt, she paused a breath in her under bindings. I did not give her time for such hesitation. Chucking my armor to the side, I advanced on her. She squealed but did not flee. I grasped her chest wrap and pulled it over her head, then pushed her lower garment over her hips. When she stood naked before me, I let my gaze peruse her body.

She shook as I stared. "Wh-what is it?"

"You're so crexing lovely," I groaned, grasping her hips and pulling her against my leathers. My cock brushed her core. "And the urge to claim you grows stronger."

"Wh-why don't you?" She placed steadying hands on my forearms. "I want you to."

I hummed in response. "We must speak before that time, but now is for something else." Letting her go, I undid my leathers and kicked them from my body. My cock, freed at last, was like an iron bar between my legs. It yearned to be inside my mate, but I held fast to my purpose.

She gasped, her eyes zeroing in on my cock. "It's huge!"

I laughed as her jaw dropped open and fought the urge to preen.

"And what is that?" Drawing closer, she brushed my crux, the extra appendage at the base. It vibrated under her touch. "Oh my god."

"It is my crux. Do human males lack one?" I watched her face curiously.

"Yeah, um. They don't have this." Her fingers traced the outer ridge, sending sparks of pleasure to my balls. "This is amazing."

I placed a hand over her seeking fingers and brought them to my mouth. "Oh, I intend it to be so."

"Cocky." She laughed, the sound ringing through the bathhouse.

"Yes, much cock." I kissed her hand. "But first, you must learn to obey."

Sage took a step back, knelt with her knees apart, bowed her head, and put her hands behind her back. "Yes, Sir," she said, a hint of defiance in her tone. "Teach me."

*Crex!* As if I hadn't been hard before, now it was enough to fuck through a wall. I had to control the situation. My little mate would not dictate her punishment. Ignoring her posture, which was the toughest challenged I'd faced yet, I turned and submerged in the bath. It only came up to my waist as I predicted, but I used the side of the tub to lean against. Then, I splashed the emerald water onto my chest and shoulders to wash away the grime. All the while, my targana stayed in her knelt posture, peeking at me from under her lashes.

"Now, Sage," I curled my fingers in a beckoning gesture, "step into the water. You are going to hand me the soap, and then, I am going to wash you. But you are not to touch me." I captured her gaze as she picked up her head. "And you are most definitely not to touch yourself. Understand?"

Her arousal spiked impossibly more, her scent like a mating call, luring me in. "Yes, I-I," she bit her lip, "I understand, Sir."

"Say it then." I took the soap from her as she placed her toes in the water. She hissed at its heat. "All the way in, and repeat my command."

"Y-you're going to wash me." The water rose to her calves as she slowly lowered down. "I c-can't touch you." The emerald bath glistened around her bare skin. "And I can't t-touch myself." She sunk to the bottom, the water level rising to her breasts which bobbed on the surface.

"Good girl," I said, holding her gaze. "That's right." She sighed at that, and I couldn't resist pushing her boundaries a bit further. "Now, hold on to the edge with both hands and spread your legs."

Her brows rose to her hairline, but she said nothing. Turning around, she did as I commanded. And crex, it tightened my gut to watch her comply. "I can't wait to fuck you like this," I whispered, letting my tongue trace the shell of her ear. "But first…"

I grasped her hips and angled her ass high, forcing her to her toes. Then, I snagged one of the silken towels, dipped it in the water and splashed on a dollop of soap from the bottle. With infinite slowness, I tended to my mate.

# 14

## Sage

I was going to implode. Self-combustion in three… two… I moaned as Brok's fingers slipped from the towel and grazed my outer pussy lips. It didn't matter how much I begged or pleaded, he refused to touch me in anyway that eased the building pressure. I thought I had understood this torment the night before, but this…this was punishment.

I wanted more.

I had the fleeting thought that I might be a masochist, but when his thick cock brushed the crease of my ass, I decided I didn't care.

"Do you understand now, targana?" His voice was gravel as he ground his cock behind me.

"Yes, Sir." I pushed back, desperate to have that hardness inside my throbbing pussy.

He groaned, and a spark of pleasure ran through me at having such an effect on him. "You understand that this body is mine?" He slapped my ass, a stinging blow even through the water. I yelped. "That your pleasure is mine?" He bent over me, and at last, pinched my aching peaks, tweaking them, rolling them and sending a zing down my spine. I moaned. "That this pussy," he angled his hips lower and brushed his huge cock against my clit, "is mine."

"Brok!" I screamed. "Yes! Yes, Sir." I squeezed the edge of the tub. "But please, fuck me!"

Grabbing my leg, he flipped me over in the water. It splashed over the rim of the bath as he drew my legs around his waist. One arm at my back, and the other at my collarbone, he said, "Look at me, my mate."

I didn't even realize I'd closed my eyes to capture every sensation. I blinked them open at his command and stared into his liquid black eyes rimmed with that captivating silver.

"I wanted us to talk, to give you time, to allow you the choice," he said, holding my gaze. Moving his hand to my throat, he squeezed lightly. "This is not a simple fucking, Sage." He bent his head lower. I could feel his breath on my face. "I'm going to claim you, possess you." He thrust his cock through my pussy lips, the head brushing my clit again. "And it will be for always. I will never let you go, and you will own my soul. Do you understand now?"

I sucked in a breath. I wanted that. My body vibrated from need, the sexual tension strung tighter than a bow string. But it was my heart, my formerly jaded heart, that cried out at his promise. I never knew how much I needed Brok, my mate, until he appeared. "Yes," I said, clutching his face in my hands. "Gods, yes, Brok. I want that more than anything."

His smile was so radiant it could rival the sun. "Then, hold on, my Truxoria, for I plan to make you mine many times before we leave this place."

"Do it," I put my arms around his neck, "please. Make me yours."

Brok did not disappoint. Shifting back so that he leaned against the tub, he picked me up and lowered me down onto his thick cock. At the same time, he sucked my right breast into his mouth while that talented tongue vibrated against the stiff peak. My pussy stretched to accommodate his massive girth, a delicious pleasure so intense it bordered on pain. But I welcomed the sting, craved it.

"More," I moaned.

Letting my nipple pop from between his lips, he hoisted me up. He pulled his cock almost all the way out of my pussy, and I held fast to his shoulders, trying to push back in place. He growled at my movements, then slammed me down.

I cried out, "Again!"

He did it again, and again. When he was seated fully inside me that appendage at the base of his cock began to vibrate. "Oh my god!" I screamed. It rubbed directly against my clit. "I can't. Brok, I can't."

"You can," he growled and sucked on my neck. "And you will." Then, he shifted me to the edge of the bath, my back cushioned by a pile of towels and my ass in the water. He cradled my hips and thrust over and over while dragging me onto his cock. That crux of his stroked and vibrated on my clit better than any sex toy.

Every stroke of his cock kissed my pussy walls. As I shook from the sensations, overwhelmed by the intensity, his cock began to vibrate too. That shattered my world. I came harder than I ever had in my life. I bucked in his grip. He thrust so deep, his thickness stretching me to the limit. He pounded into me, the vibrations working me through the waves of my orgasm. When I thought I couldn't take any more, he thrust a final time and roared his release. Gods, it filled me so good. My pussy spasmed, and I came again.

"Fuck!" I wailed to the ceiling. The bathhouse was made of stone, but I had a feeling the entire village of purple otter-aliens heard. I didn't care. I was too strung out and properly sated to worry about it.

Brok stayed inside me, still hard even though he'd come. I snickered. *Benefits of an alien warrior mate.* He lifted my body and pulled me back into the water, cradled against his chest. Slowly, he dragged his cock free, my pussy already clenching at the loss.

"Now, my targana," he cupped my chin in one large palm and captured my gaze, "We are One."

MAKING GOOD ON HIS VOW, BROK TOOK ME AGAIN IN the bath, and then a third time in the hut, which we'd be shown to after leaving the bathhouse. It was a simple square room with a door on the end that led to an outhouse style toilet, a table and two chairs in the far corner, and a pile of cozy blankets on the other end. All in all, clean and not bad.

The sun had set by the time we finished with our… activities. And after all that, I was ready to curl up under the blankets and sleep for days. But the evening had only truly begun, and my stomach growled its complaint.

*You're hungry.* Brok spoke the words in my mind having explained earlier that a Rhonar mating bond was more than physical. It allowed us to communicate thoughts to each other. It wasn't like mind-reading, thank the heavens, but more like talking—just not aloud. It had weirded me out a teeny bit, but I did my best not to let it show. After all, I'd have the rest of our lives to work it out. And that part, the forever part, was kind of amazing.

"Yes," I said, rolling onto my side and propping my head on my bent elbow. "But I don't want to get up yet."

"I can bring you food." He crouched next to me, scanning my body as if deciding between feeding me or eating me.

I pulled the blanket over me. An Earth girl could only take so much attention. "No, I want to ask the otter-aliens about the device their leader gave me, and also, I think she invited us to dinner." The sweet purple leader of the group had chittered a lot around the bonfire and mimed eating motions before delivering us to the hut. I took it to mean they'd collect us for dinner.

*Otter-aliens?* Brok thought at me.

I shrugged. *It's an Earth animal they resemble. Kind of like your florin friend is a dog-fox mix.*

He shook his head, clearly not understanding. But he didn't ask more questions, instead he sat beside me and gathered me into his lap. "I'm sorry I did not tell you more about the mate bond before." His hands massaged my scalp and worked through the tangles in my hair. "I should have resisted. You deserved a choice."

I didn't like the sadness I caught underneath his flat tone. Turning to face him, I put both my hands on his chest, one for each of his hearts. "You did. Maybe you didn't tell me *everything*." I laughed. *Like this will take some getting use to.* I pushed the thought at him like he'd instructed me before. "But I know who you are, and I have no regrets."

He sighed, taking my hands and holding them in his own. "That's just it, targana. You do not know."

A knot formed in my stomach. *What haven't you told me?* I couldn't speak that question aloud. My instincts about people were usually spot on, but it took me time to trust anyone. The fact that I could feel for him so soon proved that something beyond mere attraction had brought us together. Hell, according to him, I was the sole person in the universe who could bring back his emotions and save him from torment. So…that had to count for something, right?

As my mind spun with a jumble of chaotic ideas, each more crazier than the last, Brok held me steady. Slowly, a story about his past tumbled from his lips. He told me about his parents, his maether and paether, as he called them, and their deep love for each other that solidified their bond. His paether's dying in battle, and his maether's desperation for more children was a tale that struck my heart. I couldn't imagine losing my mom. He continued to tell me about how she'd found a new mate, and the abuse both he and his maether suffered at that male's hands. He spoke of how his friend Xelan interfered on their behalf, and how Porlax—aforementioned bastard mate of his maether—had been shunned from their society for his crimes of abuse. It didn't seem punishment enough, so I offered to kill the bastard, but Brok said that the void had already claimed him. I wasn't sure what that meant, but I didn't want to interrupt.

"I didn't save her," he hissed the words as sharp pain radiated from him.

I hugged his head to my breasts. "Brok, from what you told me you were only a child."

"So was Xelan." His hair tickled my skin, but I held him firm. *I failed her.*

And now, at last, I understood the heart of it. He didn't have to say it aloud or in my mind; it was as clear as a starry night. He thought he failed his mother, and he feared he'd fail me. Despite being a strong and capable warrior, the male in my arms was vulnerable to the idea that he was, and never would be, worthy.

My heart ached for him. "Brok, look at me."

He lifted his head, doubt swimming in his eyes.

"I can't make this better for you." I kissed his brow. "I wish I could. I would do anything to take your pain away." Another kiss over his cheek. "I'll tell you how much I value you everyday, if it will help." I brushed the hair from his face. "But you, and only you, can forgive yourself for whatever you feel you've done wrong." I held his chin in my hand. "Only you can believe that you're worthy."

He exhaled a long, harsh breath. "Thank you, Sage."

I smiled. *Of course, my mate.* Brok's answering half-smirk gave me hope that he'd begin to heal. It would be a hard road for him, but it was one I had walked. For a while after my experience with JJ, I thought I was unworthy of love. And that what I wanted was wrong. It took me time to realize that he had manipulated me, and turned what I should have owned as part of me—my desires—into something to be used.

But I'd survived, and now, I had a male who made me feel like a queen. He showed me there was power in my submission, and I would never feel bad for what I wanted again. I vowed then and there to do whatever I could to help Brok feel the same—strong, valued, and loved.

*Because I do love him.* I didn't think that part at him. But I would someday soon. He deserved that, but I wanted to be somewhere special to say it aloud. For the present, I would savor every moment we had together.

With that thought, my stomach made itself known again, growling louder than before.

Brok laughed. "Come, my Truxoria. We must find you food."

I rose from the blankets, donned my clothes, and headed out of the hut with Brok. We made our way to the bonfire pit, which the otter-aliens had coaxed into a roaring blaze. The heat felt wonderful as the night and cool winds in the valley turned the air biting.

The leader waved us over to a log beside her. She had on her crown of delicate flowers as before but had added a cloak of golden silk around her shoulders. To her people, I was certain she looked regal, but I couldn't help thinking that she was adorable. Taking a seat, I pulled the device she'd given me out of my coveralls' pocket. I was a bit guilty I hadn't spent time working on it, but I wasn't about to regret the mind-blowing hours I'd spent with Brok.

"So this," I said, turning it over in my palm, "it's a communicator?" I mimed talking with my hand.

The leader nodded. She placed a thin cylindrical object atop the device and chittered.

I eyed the thing, then I picked it up between my thumb and index finger. I hummed and turned to Brok who sat beside me. "A tool?"

He pinched the free end of it. "I believe so."

Taking a firmer grip on it, which proved tricky since it was thinner than a chopstick, I prodded the tip. It had a fine point. "Let's see what we can do with it."

Under the fire's glow, the otter-aliens gathered around. Their chitters had turned melodic as they sat on the logs and swayed together in time to their music. All the while Brok remained silent, taking in the night and watching me work. He was more relaxed there in the village than I'd yet seen him. It brought a warmth to my soul. I hoped to see him this at ease as often as possible.

*Okay, time to concentrate.* My fingers worked the cover off the device. The tubulars inside were thin and old, almost like ancient wiring from Earth. But I didn't see any discernible cause for concern like fraying or cracking. I found one loose red line that had coiled around a spool in the opposite direction. I clucked my tongue. "It can't be that easy. Can it?"

I decided to find out. Using my thin tool, I carefully looped the line away from the spool, then flipped it to follow the same path as the others. Once that was achieved, I reconnected the cover, flipped the device over, and…

"I have no idea how to turn it on." I searched the panels for a button, or lever, or switch. "Nothing."

The leader having gone to make the rounds with her people, returned to the empty spot beside us. As I'd worked others had come to observe us, but I hardly noticed them except as passing forms. I had been too focused on fixing the device. Now that I was close to possibly achieving my goal, I brought my attention to the otter-aliens once more. I turned to the leader and motioned to the device, then smiled and shrugged.

She chittered at me as if in question.

Taking a chance, I nodded at her and handed it to her.

Her cute little nose wriggled, which shook her whiskers. Then, she chittered more excitedly than before. Pressing in the center of the cover with both thumbs, the device flared to life. A white glow emitted around the edge, and it gave off a pop-pop. And then…

The otter-alien leader stood before us, device in hand. "Do you learn now?"

"Holy shit!" I shouted.

It wasn't my proudest moment. But I was so surprised, I stumbled off the log. And that was how I had made my first official introduction to a species of otter-aliens.

# 15

## Brok

I HELPED MY MATE SIT BACK ON THE LOG. I DIDN'T blame her for her shock. I'd sputtered the drink the beings had given me into the dirt at my feet. I hadn't doubted Sage's abilities to fix the device; I simply never imagined the primitive machine would work.

"You can talk," Sage said, staring with her lovely green eyes at the leader.

A laugh bubbled from between the being's pink mouth, its whiskers shaking with the movement. "Of course, starlings, we speak. You not understand us."

"We apologize." I bowed my head at the leader. "We knew you were intelligent, and you've treated us kindly, but we did not think we'd be able to converse with you."

"We happy this." The leader smiled warmly. "I be Nayla. And they, my people."

I put a hand to to the center of my chest, according Nayla the respect she deserved as leader. "It is an honor to meet you. I am Brok, and this is my mate, Sage."

"Hi." Sage waved, a little shyly, at the leader.

"We honor met. But we not know you as friend first." Her gaze flicked to Sage, then back at me. "Your mate, no worry. But you, we see, and worry."

The translation device made communication possible, but Nayla's words were still difficult to piece together. Sage spoke up, "You mean, you've seen Brok before?"

"No him." The leader scrunched up her muzzle. "Same, but gray."

I froze. "You've seen beings with gray skin that look like me?"

"Yes, like you. Big." She rose from the log and raised her paws in the air. "They come. They take."

I understood why my friend from earlier had tensed when I spoke about leading us to the fuel source. The Versaken had already been here. The scourge of my kind, our most fearsome enemy and our greatest shame, they destroyed, pillaged, and rampaged without mercy. If these beings had encountered them, I was surprised they were still alive.

"You've fought them?" I asked, my hearts stuttering behind my ribs. I did not want to imagine these kind people warring with the Versaken.

"No, no." Nayla flapped her paws. "They not get us. We hidden here. They not want valley." She motioned toward the mountains. "They steal there."

I glanced over her head at the mountain far too close to this valley. If the Versaken had come, then these beings were in danger.

Sage put a gentle hand on my shoulder. "You know what's she's talking about, don't you?"

"Yes, targana." I sighed and scrubbed a roughened palm over my neck. "They are Versaken. The species that came to be from the fallen Rhonar."

Her eyes widened as she gasped. "You mean…" She switched to our private mind speak. *If you fall prey to the void, you become…something else?*

I wrapped an arm around her waist and drew her in close. She was so draving smart, but I would not let her worry. *That will never happen to me, my Truxoria. You have saved me from that fate.* She moved her hand to my chest and put her head on my shoulder. I took strength form our embrace and focused on the leader once more. "What is your kind called?"

Nayla straightened her spine, sitting higher. "We the gyorpin, rightful people, and protectors of planet Gyorp."

The laughter bubbled inside Sage. With her leaning against me I could feel it shake her chest, but she held it tight. *I don't want to insult her*, she thought at me. *But that name is so funny sounding in translation.*

I didn't disagree. Yet, I found the name's likeness to our florin allies—and their appearance, now that I thought on it—too similar to ignore. "Are you aware of the florin?"

"Florin." She rose from the bench with a jump. "Yes. Florin our cousins."

I stared around the bonfire at the gyorpin as if seeing them for the first time. Although bigger than the florin with no tails and a thick pelt instead of fur, they had clear similarities in the muzzle and whiskers that I couldn't ignore. "Can you contact them?"

Nayla nodded. "Yes, yes. Take time. They far."

I had deduced as much, since none of the florin had answered my prior calls. If they couldn't hear me, then they wouldn't come, no matter how far they could travel between dimensions. I hoped the gyorpin had another way to summon them. If the Versaken were on this planet, then we were all in danger—and we'd need help.

Sage cocked a brow at me. *Going to clue me in.*

I laughed aloud. My mate saw everything. It would be a challenge to surprise her. But I'd enjoy trying. *Later.*

She sighed but nodded.

Meanwhile Nayla beckoned to her companions, waving for them to come forward. Two gyorpin carrying trays of meats, fruits, and loaves of bread, and one holding a stack of bowls, strode before her. She chose a piece of each food and placed them all in a bowl, then gave this to Sage. She did it again and handed the next to me. We both nodded our thanks, waiting for her to take a bowl for herself. But she made one for every gyorpin around the bonfire, before at last taking the remains.

The act raised my respect for her to new heights. A leader who put her people first was a person worth following. When all present had their fill of food and drink, Nayla rose again and addressed the group. "Starlings Brok and Sage, honored guests." Her gazed traveled to the mountain that was bathed in the light of the rising moon. "Tomorrow we help them. They need glava. Get home."

I caught the eye of the gyorpin I had spoken to earlier. He nodded at me. It must have been he who informed Nayla of our plight, perhaps even convinced her to aid us. I inclined my head toward him in gratitude. He raised a cup and drank deeply. I did the same.

"We not see gray men. They not see us. We safe." Stomping her hind paws on the ground, she lowered her voice an octave. "They see, we perish."

The gyorpin stomped their paws in answer with cries of, "No see! No see!"

Sage raised her head and cast a worried look around the bonfire. She whispered to me, "Brok, we can't put these people in danger."

"I know," I said firmly in agreement. *But we cannot embarrass their leader either.* I sighed, weariness settling in my bones at last. I had not slept for several solar days, pushing the limits of my endurance. *We will come up with a plan tomorrow.*

As we sat in the comfort of the gyorpin's fire, I pondered how to keep our new friends from danger.

THE SUN ROSE TOO EARLY THE NEXT MORNING. I HAD passed the night filled with visions of Versaken monsters tearing through the gyorpin's village. Several times I had held Sage tighter, trying to banish the nightmares. She'd whimpered in her sleep, plagued no doubt by similar sights.

When we approached the leader about the trek to the mountain, she would not be convinced to remain behind. "You friend. We help."

"If the Versaken are in the mountain, it would be best for me to sneak in alone than to bring a group of your people." I motioned to the assembled party. At least a dozen gyorpin stood at attention in rows of varying shades of purple.

Sage caught my words. "Alone?" she asked innocently, but the bite to her question was not lost on me.

Outnumbered by the females, I chose my words with care. "Yes, targana." I stroked a hand through her hair the way I knew she liked. "If you remain here with the gyorpin—"

Removing my hand from her hair, she dropped it at my side and clenched her fist. "If you know what's good for you, you'll stop right there."

I blew out a frustrated breath. "Going in with more increases the risk of being seen."

"Agreed." Sage turned to the leader. "Which is why the gyorpin should remain in the village and try to contact help," she spun back to me, "while *we* go to the mountain and get the fuel."

I pinched the bridge of my nose. *Celestia, give me strength.*

*I heard that.* She narrowed her eyes at me.

"Fine," I conceded, knowing I'd have to physically restrain my mate before she'd agree to stay behind. Although a tempting thought, I'd rather her aroused in restraints than waiting to stab me.

"I knew you'd see it my way." She smiled and patted my arm.

I grumbled but said nothing.

Nayla chimed in. "Not right. We friends."

Sage took the leader's paw and held it. "We are friends. And that's why we need your help." Crouching to eye level, she met her on equal footing. "Will you contact the florin? With them, we can relay a message to Brok's brothers, and the Rhonar can rid your planet of these enemies."

She looked to me for confirmation. I crossed my arms over my armor and thought to her, *Yes, we will not allow the Versaken to plague this land.*

Nayla's whiskers twitched. She did not seem wholly convinced. Glancing back at her people, she let out a strained murmur. "If you wish. We stay. Florin call."

"Thank you!" Sage shook the paw in her hand and spun the leader around in a circle. That helped to lighten the tension in the air.

"You silly," Nayla said, but it was a lighthearted jest. "Go now. Be safe."

With our bags newly packed and our new friends safe in their village, Sage and I headed up the valley stairs. The gyorpin guards watched as we went, and Nayla waved at us from the ground below. It was with heavy hearts we left that small slice of sweetness. It was a welcome reprieve from the obstacles we had encountered.

"I hope they'll be okay." Sage glanced over her shoulder, but as we walked the mountain path once more, the valley was already hidden from view. "And that we'll see them again."

"As do I, my mate." I grasped her arm for a moment's pause to kiss her forehead. "But no matter what, we will achieve our goal, and then my brathers and I will make this planet safe for our friends."

She squared her shoulders visibly and stood taller. "Right. Then, let's do this."

Set to our purpose, we hiked toward the mountain. We made fast progress as the terrain was even on the pass and inclined gradually. The gyorpin had told us of a side path, hidden in the boulders on the eastern rim that would skirt around the main entrance, and take us into the heart of the mountain. With luck, we'd never run into the Versaken and be able to acquire the fuel we needed—a substance our friends called glava—and return to our ship.

Yet, I didn't believe in luck. So I sent up a silent plea to the sacred divine. She had been kind to me of late, and I prayed I remained in her good graces to see this mission through.

We found the hidden path by mid-morning. It was covered in rocks, not the smooth terrain of the main pass. But it looked unused, which gave me hope we'd remain hidden from enemy eyes. "Stay close to me." I put a steadying hand on my mate's hips and bade her go ahead of me. I did not want her slipping on this uneven ground and injuring herself. "Go slow."

"I will." She had grown quiet as we'd journeyed on, and I worried over her silence. But the fierce determination emanating from her was to be praised. So I did not speak of it, allowing her to concentrate on our objective.

The path proved a challenge for my brave mate, slowing our steps to a crawl, but we reached the doorway to the mountain by the mid-day. Before we slipped inside, we took meal bars from our back and choked them down with gulps of water.

"Ugh, when we get out of here, promise me we'll never eat those things again." Brushing her mouth with the back of her hand, she took another swig from our water canteen.

I chuckled, elated that her mood had eased enough to joke. "It is a promise then."

"Good." She snagged one more sip, then placed the water back in her pack. "I'm so ready to get this done."

"As am I." We entered the doorway and picked our steps with care as we moved further inward. The mountain had a rotten smell to it that assailed the senses. I struggled to breath without gagging.

Sage coughed and pulled up her shirt to cover the bottom half of her face. She mumbled behind her improvised covering, "That's horrible."

I nodded, holding my nose to avoid the worst of it.

The gyorpin informed us that the glava was a gelatinous yellowish substance and gave us a container to carry it in. I had that strapped to my side. We needed merely a flagon's worth to infuse into our ship's tank. The substance was that powerful a fuel source.

We hadn't gone far, when Sage squealed internally, pushing her thoughts to me. *That's it!*

I followed her arm where she pointed and saw the yellow-green tint at the base of the far wall. It had to be the glava. A pinging sensation rippled along my spine. I had discovered in my long years of battle that nothing went one hundred percent to plan, and this...this was too easy.

Not wanting to alarm my mate, I headed for the glava and quickly scooped the container full. Capping it and replacing it at my side, I grabbed Sage's hand and picked up the pace out of the mountain.

"Whoa, Brok," she said, taking two steps for each one of mine. "Is the place on fire?"

My urge to keep her safe warred with my instinct to tell her the truth. I opted for a middle ground. "It's too quiet."

Glancing around, she didn't slow but her hand tensed in mine. "You're right." She sped up, matching my stride.

We exited the mountain and trekked the hidden path back the way we'd come. The sun was still high in the sky, having passed its zenith not long ago. Our time in the mountain had been a handful of clicks. Yet, the tension in my muscles would not dissipate.

When we traded the hidden path for the main pass, my lungs tightened. It was then I heard a noise all too familiar and filled with dread—the din of battle. I shifted my pack and the glava-filled container to the ground and grabbed my ax. Sage asked no questions, chucking her pack and claiming the tool she favored from her thigh strap.

"Assess first," I warned her. I pointed two fingers at my eyes, then to the directions where the sounds originated. "And follow my lead."

Her mouth tightened in a hard line. *I will.*

As we stalked silently down the passage toward the unknown, I had but one thought in my mind. *No one shall harm my mate.*

# 16

# Sage

My palms sweat, my knees trembled, and I had to pee. *Why did you drink so much water?* My mom used to beg me not to drink on our road trips. Earth had few inhabitable spots anymore. Some people lived in the wilds, refusing to accept the global government and its technological advancements. But they were scattered and considered outliers. Most of the world's population was condensed into self-contained cities. Yet on the edge of each city, before the boundaries crossed into the outlands, tiny slices of paradise dotted the landscape —trees.

I'd loved visiting the woodlands as a child, watching the leaves change colors at different times of the year. It was why the crimson and gray forest had charmed me, well, before its inhabitants wanted to eat me, of course. Yet, even after this incredible journey, which my friends and sisters were never going to believe, I came to the one conclusion that resonated within me.

*I would change nothing.* I didn't send that thought to Brok, but I knew he felt it all the same. It echoed in him too. For all the challenges had brought us together, and that was worth everything.

I steeled my resolve. If we could get beyond this last hurdle, we'd make it home. We had to. I wanted a lifetime with Brok, to introduce him to my family, to show him my favorite old holo-vids, to dance with him in zero gravity. I ached with that desire for our future.

Creeping up to the scene of the battle, the air rushed from me. The path curved sharply downward at this level, an area that I remembered well from climbing up it, and flattened out several feet below. On that lower ground, gray-skinned males as tall and wide as Brok attacked with serrated swords and knives. Purple hides fought back, but they didn't stand a chance against the stronger opponents.

Brok turned to me, horror written on his face. "They won't survive."

"We have to do something." Tears stung my eyes.

"We will, targana." He threaded his fingers through mine. "I cannot stand idle and watch their suffering."

I chewed on my bottom lip and sent to him, *Neither can I.*

Tension radiated from him. I knew he wanted me to stay behind, his burning need to protect me was a powerful force between us. His gaze scanned the battleground. We saw the same hopeless numbers. He tucked me into his side, glancing down at me once more. "We won't win."

I nodded, my voice barely more than a whisper. "I know."

His body vibrated. "Don't ask me to lead you to your death, my Truxoria. I cannot do it."

"I would never ask you to do that," I said, gripping his shoulders and pulling him close. "But I *will* stand beside you."

"My little warrior mate." He nuzzled his chin atop my head. "I wanted more time, but whether now or a hundred years from now, I'd feel the same." Looking into my eyes, he rested his forehead against mine. "You are my everything." Then, he kissed me deeply, holding me tight as if the universe shrunk to just him and me. It wasn't a goodbye kiss, but one filled with love. When we broke apart, he whispered against my lips, "We are One."

I held his head in place and nuzzled his nose. "I love you, Brok."

"And I love you, Sage." His words ran over my soul like a desert flower watered by an oasis.

It was impossible to pull apart, but somewhere inside us we found the strength—together. Turning as a unit, we brandished our weapons. Brok's energy shield flared a brilliant blue against the planet's orange sunlight. And with a cry, we plunged into battle.

The first Versaken we encountered was half a foot taller than Brok. I swung low, striking the male's shins with my astro-wrench while Brok aimed high, his ax cutting through the enemy's armor like butter. The male fell where he stood and didn't move again. I didn't have time to consider my actions. I focused only on the next step, the next strike. My goal was to save my friends. The time for regret could come later.

The second Versaken saw us coming. He braced his boots into the ground, standing like a marble statue. The sickening part of this enemy was that they looked like Brok. Same tattooed arms, although their patterns were white instead of the brilliant metallic silver of the Rhonar, and faded into the skin. Brok had told me that those symbols, their katra, were formed from a malleable material they poured on their arms when reaching malehood and then molded with their kedara, essentially their energy, to form the patterns. He had said the space on his wrists was reserved for his mate, and he couldn't wait to form the perfect symbol for me. I felt sick staring at our enemy's katra, knowing it to be the ghost of another life.

Although sadness filled me, it did not stop me from attacking. These Versaken were lost to the void and out to kill the gyorpins. I wouldn't let that happen without a fight. Brok charged the male, throwing his shield at the enemy's chest to drive him back. His move gave me a chance to slide in low and slice at the back of the legs. The male howled and reared around with his curved blade, striking Brok in the shoulder. Blood poured over Brok's arm, staining his katra red.

I screamed.

Scrambling to my feet to get to Brok, I didn't see the arm swinging toward me in time. Brok shouted and threw his shield at me. But before I even registered the attack, a furry mass of dusty rose fur blinked into focus before my eyes. It changed the momentum of the Versaken's attack so that the curved blade met Brok's shield and reverberated off it. The enemy stumbled and was cut down.

"What the—"

The creature, which my brain slowly registered as Brok's florin friend, snapped his tiny fingers under my nose. A feeling of urgency hit me, like it was being pushed into me from an outside force. It had my feet racing and my body ducking low without thinking. Then, the little guy popped out of sight.

Brok caught up to me and grabbed my wrist with his injured arm. He tugged me to his side, even as he covered the wound with his free hand, a wad of silken material in his palm. I kicked into another gear at the sight of his blood. I put a hand to his waist and guided him to lean against a nearby boulder. Then, I moved his hand away to assess the damage.

"What's happening out there?" I asked as a distraction. I prodded the flesh around the injury site, glad to see the bleeding was slow and the wound shallow. "Where did the florin come from?

He hissed as I tied a new piece of gyorpin silk I'd procured from my coveralls' pocket around his wound. "Nayla and the others must have made contact with the florin." Bangs and shouts crashed all around us, the chaotic sounds of battle a thunderous cacophony. "But look there." He pointed toward the lower portion of the path at the base of the mountain. "The tide of the battle is changing."

I squinted to see the shapes in the distance. It took a few seconds for my eyes to make out the details, but bronzed skin gleamed in the orange sunlight. "Rhonar!" I cheered, whipping my head around to shoot Brok a smile. "They're here."

His answering grin sent my heart soaring. "Yes, my mate." Draping his uninjured arm across my shoulders, he held me tight. "My brathers have come."

THE BATTLE DIDN'T LAST LONG AFTER THE RHONAR arrived. With their fighter ships flying a tight formation overhead and their warriors overpowering the Versaken on the ground, the enemy had nowhere to escape. Brok and I did our part and fought anyone within range, but we didn't leave the boulder where I'd tended to his wound. He'd claimed it was already healing.

I'd scoffed at that. "I don't care if you're the biggest, baddest warrior in the whole damn universe." I'd swung my astro-wrench into the back of a Versaken male while our florin friend, popped in and out of sight, scratching at the enemy. Brok's ax had delivered the final blow. "You're injured, and we're staying here."

It couldn't have been more than fifteen minutes that passed, but it had felt like a lifetime. Now, Brok and I stood on the higher ground of the mountain pass, waiting for his brathers to finish checking the wounded. I spotted the gyorpin leader on a nearby ridge.

"Nayla!" I shouted to her, so relieved to find her alive. "Over here!"

Her purple hide had faded slightly. She wore no adornments, only a simple belt that housed several weapons. Her paws were covered in blood, but she wiped them on the rocks as she walked toward us. Two of her gyorpin guards hovered on either side of her. I recognized one as the male Brok had spoken to when we first met them.

"Starling friends!" she exclaimed as she got closer. "You safe."

"Yes." I met her half way to help her up the hill. When she extended her paw, I patted it and then held fast to guide her the remaining distant. "So are you. I'm so glad."

Brok leaned on the boulder, but straightened when we approached. "Nayla." He bowed to her and each of her guards in turn, then he rose to his full height. "How are your people?"

"Much loss." Her sad words were uttered low, her whiskers drooping. "Such waste."

Her sorrow hit me in the chest as fierce as any physical blow. I sat at Brok's feet and motioned for her to follow. "Sit, please. And tell us, what happened?"

Scanning the grounds for a heartbeat, she sighed and plopped down. Brok followed but crouched on his haunches, staying alert. Nayla's guards did not sit, but she motioned them to step back, giving us more space. "I blame. My fault."

"No, that's not true," I said, the fierceness of my conviction evident in my tone. "The only ones to blame are the monsters who attacked you."

Her eyes watered and her antennas bent inward. "I leader. I command. We follow you."

Brok leaned forward, watching Nayla with sympathy written across his face. "You followed us?"

"Yes, follow. Make sure safe." Soft sniffles broke from her, and my heart shattered into a million pieces. If I'd harbored any regret in fighting the Versaken, I didn't now. She waved her tiny paws. "But they see. They find us."

"We are sorry, Nayla." Brok held one of her paws in his large hands and gave a gentle squeeze. "Thank you for caring so much about us."

I fell more in love with him at that moment. He tended to her suffering and grief with care and understanding. Let anyone call him stoic again and I'd have something to say about it. I placed my hand atop Nayla's paw still in Brok's hand. "We're very grateful to you and your people."

As if our words had an effect, she rose and nodded to us. "Thank you, starling friends." Swiping at her eyes, she brightened a bit. "We strong. We heal." Her guards came forward, and she turned to leave us.

I put a staying hand on her arm. "Wait, take this." I took out my astro-wrench that was strapped to my thigh and filthy from battle. Wiping it against my coveralls, I attempted to clean it, but it bore the stains. Still, it meant more to me than trinkets, and I hoped Nayla understood my intention. I placed it atop her outstretched paws. It was too big for her, but a wide smile crossed her muzzle. "I know it's a little awkward, and you probably don't know what it is, but well…" I scratched at my ear. My cheeks flushed with embarrassment. "It's my favorite tool, and you know, I fix things, so…"

Nayla clutched it to her chest like it was a precious jewel. "You give gift. I keep always."

"Oh, it's not that big a deal." I held my hands up as if to shake off the gesture and dug a booted toe in the dirt.

"It special. You treasure." She hooked the astro-wrench to her belt. With speed I didn't know she possessed, she wrapped her paws around my waist and hugged me tight. When she leaned back to stare up at me, she added, "I treasure."

I hugged her back, feeling my eyes grow glassy. "Okay."

Releasing me, she headed toward her guards who flanked her on either side. This time when she walked away, she glanced over her shoulder with a smile and a wave.

Brok, who had observed the interaction without comment, rose beside me and drew me into his embrace. Speaking in our special way, he said, *That was very kind of you, targana.* His lips brushed my neck as he leaned over me and whispered, "You are my treasure."

My heart squeezed, reformed and tended to by my mate. *My mate.* I spoke the words to him with all the love inside me. The idea of that still amazed me, and hopefully, always would—my mate. I never believed in fate. If the universe had plans, surely they didn't include foolish humans from an isolated blue planet in the cosmos. I'd thought, if I wanted something, I had to get it through hard work, not chance. But Brok?

I couldn't have dreamed up a male more perfect for me in all the endless galaxies. I certainly wouldn't have imagined we'd wind up together. And a bond that allowed us to speak to each other in our minds? No, that was the stuff of fantasy, not reality.

For old me.

So, I gave Nayla my astro-wrench not only to keep as a memory of me, but to let go of who I was before. That woman no longer existed. Sure I'd still fix anything mechanical I could get my hands on—I was already dreaming about taking apart that fuel tank back on the ship. But I wasn't going to be that jaded person anymore. I'd take life as I found it.

Brok's breath in my hair set my heart racing. A smile stretched my lips wide.

And sometimes, I'd trust that the universe might have my back after all.

# 17

## Brok

THE GYORPINS HAD GIVEN TOO MUCH, SACRIFICING THEIR lives for strangers they barely knew. Yet, I admired their courage. I'd take nothing from them that would risk dishonoring that bravery.

Still as I held my mate in my arms, the sight of Commander Torian in the mountain pass was a welcome relief. He scaled the ridge toward us, his sharp eyes shifting to my mate then to me. "Fair meet, Brokdar," he said formally, the subtle chastisement in his tone evident. Yet, he held out his arm for a warrior's clasp. "The brathers and I feared we would not see you again."

I clasped his forearm, inclining my head in an acknowledgment of his rank. "For a time, I thought the same."

He hummed his agreement but tightened his hold a fraction. "Do not think I've forgotten your earlier insubordination." Yanking me forward, he flexed a hand to my uninjured shoulder and eyed my wounded one. "But I am glad you are well."

"Thank you, Tor." I switched to his nickname. He was my commanding officer, but he was also of my *Brather*—the sacred bond of chosen family. He'd understand my actions, but he was owed an explanation. "I'm afraid I had to act quickly, and I ask your forgiveness."

He raised a brow. "Instead of my permission?"

"Yes, my mate's life was at stake." I heard Sage's gasp and tugged her to my side, my arm around her shoulders. "Meet my Truxoria, Sage."

"Ah hi!" She waved at Tor, then stuck out her hand as if unsure what to do.

Tor glanced at me, and I nodded. Wrapping his fingers around her palm in the gentlest touch I'd ever seen from him, he shook it exactly once up and down. "Fair meet, Sage. It is an honor."

"Thanks," she drew her hand back slowly and hooked it into the pocket of her coveralls, "you too."

"Well now, this is a much better party!" a voice from over the ridge floated to us. I recognized it immediately…and groaned. Miach's head appeared from over the ridge, the glow in his amber eyes apparent even from a distance. He was our greatest healer with the ability to see a person's injury or ailment just by proximity. But his inquisitive nature grated my nerves. "No cries of pain up here."

"That's in poor taste, Healer." Tor's words fell with the weight of an avalanche as he used the male's title.

Miach bowed his head. "Apologies, Commander. I forget where the line between dark humor and simply darkness lies." A ghost of pain whispered across his eyes, but I blinked and it disappeared. He stretched his back with a crack. "Ah, but there's more to be tended here." His gaze zeroed in on me like a predator targeting prey.

I bristled. "No, Miach. I am fine."

Sage's head spun from me to the healer and back. "Wait, can he help you?"

"And who is this beauty?" Moving with that blazing fast speed of his, he stepped within a yauna of my mate.

I growled at him in warning. Another step and *he'd* need healing.

He held up his hands in surrender. "All right, no reason to get up in arms, Brok." Ignoring me, he turned his attention to her and bowed. "I am Miach, Healer of the Rhonar, and it is my pleasure to meet you, Terran female."

When he reached for her hand, I struck him in the gut with my fist.

"Brok!" Sage yelped, and pushed at my side. "That wasn't necessary."

"Oh, it was *my mate*," I said the last words loudly to emphasize my point. "*He* needs to learn."

Miach laughed, straightening after my blow. "Still as strong as ever then. That's good." He clamped onto my injured shoulder. I grunted. "Glad to see the isolation of solo travel hasn't weakened your senses." His fingers wrapped around my wound, and my eyes watered. "Now, let's fix this."

I cursed him in silence as he pushed his healing energy into me. It flared an orange glow up and down my arm.

He hissed. "Damn. That stings worse than I imagined. If you'd simply let me help, it wouldn't be so difficult."

"Your healing is invasive," I said through gritted teeth.

"Yeah well, it's no fun for me either." When the muscles began to knit together, he sighed. "And here I thought it'd be better up on the hill." His eyes cut to the lower portion of the mountain pass below, darkening with his countenance. "Instead of down there."

A tremor ran through his hand still connected to me. I forgot that for all the healer's bravado, he didn't have it easy. His abilities were invaluable in a battle, but they came at a cost. And he suffered that price. He pulled his hand away, and I mumbled a begrudging, "Thank you."

His eyes widened in mock surprise. The bastard was caught by the hunger, our first biological stage. He couldn't feel a damn thing, just the aching craving that could never be sated. Yet, he insisted on these displays of emotion. And I realized with astonishment I could *feel* that annoyance. He didn't just bother me for what I deemed to be inappropriate behavior for a Rhonar warrior, he actually *annoyed* me. I'd only had emotions back for a few days, but to feel them toward one of my brathers was…life-changing.

"And now that you're all better, introduce me properly." Miach motioned toward my mate.

I smiled at my new found knowledge, and this time, I'd show her off as the jewel she was. "This is Sage," I said, drawing her under the protection of my arm once more. "She is a Terran engineer, and my hearts beat for her alone."

"Well said." Miach shot me a toothy grin. It was a poor facsimile of a genuine smile. Even if he aggravated me to no end, I hoped he'd one day have cause for a real smile. "Commander," he said, turning with a flourish to Tor, "my work here is done. I'm heading back to the ship for some well earned relaxation time." He flicked a hand toward all of us in turn. "Until next time."

Sage's green eyes twinkled as she watched the healer leave. "Well, he's a handful, isn't he?"

I snorted, ready to give my assessment, but Tor beat me to it. "That is an understatement." He shook his head. "Back to matters at hand." Motioning for Sage and I to follow, he began the trek over the ridge. "The ships are waiting on the eastern fields."

I kept Sage close to me as we walked a step behind Tor. "How did you end up finding us?"

"After you were lost through the wormhole, we concluded the Versaken might know of your location, since the weapon to puncture space was their creation. We," he glanced over his shoulder, his brows drawing low and his eyes narrowing, "acquired one of their pilots."

Sage gasped. "You tortured him?"

"We questioned him." Tor waved aside her concern. He wouldn't understand my mate's tender feelings. He had none that remained. "After he confessed to the weapon opening to the Meta Sector, we sent a scouting ship and our florin allies to begin the search." He rolled his head along his shoulders, popping his neck. "Not many of us were left in this sector, but one picked up your long-range beacon. Good of you to set that off." He smirked at me. "We used the enemy's weapon to arrive here. But we had difficulty tracking you on the planet's surface. Then, the florin alerted us that they'd received a message from these creatures, their cousins, the..." Snapping his fingers, he turned to Sage. "What are they called again?"

"Gyorpin," she supplied, an edge to her voice.

My mate and I valued our new friends, and while my Rhonar brathers protected the innocent, we did not always understand their true worth. With my emotions,

I'd learned so much more, and my gut clenched at how much my brathers lacked.

*He needs a mate*, she thought silently at me.

My arm tightened around her. *All of them do. More than I realized.*

Sage put her arm at my waist, squeezing me back as we walked.

Tor continued, "Yes, they pointed us to you. Although, I would like to know what the Versaken are doing on this planet."

Sage hummed. "Maybe they didn't intend for the wormhole generator to be a weapon."

We all stopped in our tracks at her words. Tor spoke first, "What do you mean?"

"Well, if they're harvesting the resources on this planet, and trying to attack you, and you're all hanging around Earth," she snapped her fingers as if solving a puzzle, "then it stands to reason they'd need a method to travel between the two planets quickly." She shrugged. "What's faster than a wormhole?"

"Nothing." I let out a slow breath. The implications of our enemy's actions hit me like laser fire. Why did we not see the obvious earlier? *Because we always see weapons, not tools.* I tensed. "They could have an army surrounding Earth before we knew what hit us."

Straightening his spine, Tor barked out orders to the com unit on his wrist for any ships in atmosphere to leave immediately. "We borrowed one of their wormhole generators. We need to use it to get back to Earth. Now."

THE RUN TO OUR SHUTTLE CRAFTS, AND THE REMAINING battle cruiser that awaited us in space, left my poor mate breathless. We'd hardly had time to strap in before the shuttle lifted off and raced for the cruiser. My fighter was left behind, the glava we collected never even put to use.

Sage sighed as we departed the shuttle and stepped onto the battle cruiser's docking bay. I wanted to show her around the impressive ship, but with the potential threat to Earth, we had to use the enemy's technology and take the wormhole back as soon as possible. I strapped her into a passenger seat, next to the viewer that gave a look into the blackness of space, and then I took the chair beside her. I was a fighter pilot, and until a space battle began, my brathers would not have need of me.

"Do you really think they'll send an army to Earth?" Her beautiful eyes were as round as the moons of my home world.

"I don't know, targana." I took her hand, threading my fingers through hers and laying our joined hands on her lap. "But we will protect your planet, no matter the cost."

She chewed on her lower lip and went silent. I longed to comfort her. But the ship's countdown began, and within three clicks, we shot through the wormhole. It was a smoother ride in the enormous battle cruiser than it had been in my smaller space fighter, but not smooth enough for my mate. Her face looked almost as green as her eyes, and she breathed in and out in small puffs through her nose.

"Almost through it," I said patting our joined hands with my free one.

When we emerged in the space surrounding Earth, my muscles fired. Bunching under my skin, I made ready internally for battle. But the viewer showed...nothing. No Versaken ships, no laser fire, just the blue and green surface of the planet below.

I rose from the seat and helped my mate free of the straps. Taking her hand again, I guided her to the bridge. Tor stood at the commander's post, staring through the main viewer and seeing the same sights I had. "Commander?" I called to him as my brothers all turned to face us. "Has the sensors picked up any Versaken vessels?"

"None," he said, raking a hand through his hair. He muttered under his breath but loud enough for Rhonar ears to pick up, "What are they up to?"

Sage walked onto the bridge, striding over to Tor. "Well, this is good news for now, no?"

I followed and pulled her into my arms from behind her. "It is, targana." Catching Tor's eye, I silently dared him to argue.

"Yes." He lowered his chin to stare down at her. "Of course, it is." He picked his head up to look at me. "Why not give her a tour of the ship and rest awhile. Free quarters are in section four."

"Wait," Sage cried and tugged on my arm. "I need to speak to my sister, my friend, my superiors on the moonbase." The ache in her voice had me holding her tighter. "I have to let them know I'm okay!"

"We'll put a call through immediately for you," he said to her, then shifted, an uncomfortable stare between her and me. "But I'm afraid we have some things to discuss before you speak with your fellow Terrans."

"What things?" Her body stiffened in my hold.

"Please." He held out his palms face up to her, the Rhonar sign for patience or mercy, depending on the circumstances. I snickered as Tor might have been asking for both. My mate was fierce in her indignation. "I vow to explain it all to you, but give me a few spans. There is much to be done and little time to do it." He raised a brow. "You may clean up and have a private rest with your mate until then."

Sage's eyes turned to me, and I let her see my desire in them. I'd never regret having time alone with my mate, even if that meant my curiosity over Tor's words lingered.

She sighed. "I suppose I don't have a choice."

Laughing, I spun her in my arms. "Come, my mate, it is not as bad as all that." Kissing her for all my brathers to witness, I added in our private talk, *I can think of many ways to distract you for a time.*

The blush that rose on her neck and cheeks was my goal. *Well, when you put it that way.*

Guiding her from the command bridge, I could feel my brathers' envious stares. Although they had no emotions in them, they needed what I had.

I definitely had to travel to a Celestian temple soon to give thanks. But not now, and not before I took care of my mate.

## Sage

My mom liked to say that patience was a virtue, but I liked to think it was a poison. It seeped inside you as dangerous as any toxin and turned your insides to mush. At least that's what waiting felt like to me. There was one thing that could help…

"You *have* to show me the engine room on this baby!" I bounced on the balls of my feet, excitement zipping through me at all the mechanical marvels an advanced ship of this size had to have.

"*That's* what you want to do?" Brok's incredulous tone hinted at what *he* wanted to do.

I laughed. I couldn't help it. "I mean I want to do *that* too." I looped my arm through his, catching a whiff of myself as I did. "And shower for sure." I snorted out the smell. "But first, the engines!"

"I can deny you nothing, targana." He let loose a suffering sigh. "Let us see them then."

Engineering was the stuff of my dreams. The engines were encapsulated by an enormous energy shield that was both created by and designed to protect the machines. I drooled. "This is amazing!" The clicks and beeps of the various instruments had me humming along with them. I itched to get my hands on some tools and pry it all apart to see what made it tick. "I need to study the schematics. Please tell me I can see them."

"The computer will have them," Brok said, watching me with sheer joy written across his face. "We can access them from private quarters." His tone dropped at this last part, and it sent a jolt to my core.

As much as I wanted to study the most epic machinery I'd ever seen, my mate was far more appealing. I cast him a glance that was all business. "Shower first."

He strode toward me. "Yes, we will get clean," he whispered in my ear, then ran his tongue along my neck, "and then dirty again."

I shuddered.

The walk toward the empty quarters took forever as Brok mind spoke all the things he wanted to do to me. As he slid the door open to allow us inside, I was wet with desire.

"Brok," I moaned into his mouth as he picked me up by my hips and carried me into the bathroom. We stripped quickly, tearing at each other's clothes. I sobered a little when he turned on the shower, and it sprayed us with that weird glittery-black goop. It coated every inch of my skin, working efficiently to clean my body, but feeling like slime nonetheless. By the time the foam followed, dissolving the gel-slime, I was ready to be done with the shower.

I searched every square inch of my body to make sure none of the goop remained. Brok laughed at my antics, before his eyes turned hot. "Allow me to help you." He picked me up and threw me onto the bed. Then, he rechecked every part of me with his tongue.

"Now, Brok." I tugged at his hair, which was currently tickling the inside of my thighs.

The silver rim of his black eyes gleamed wickedly. Moving with lightning quickness, he rose and flipped me onto my stomach. Two slaps to my ass cheeks had me groaning into the pillow. "That's for not asking me correctly." He grabbed my hips and pulled me up to my hands and knees. "Now, tell me what you want the right way before I decide to punish you."

"Brok!" Another slap landed on my ass. "I mean, Sir! Please, take me."

He leaned over my back and tweaked my nipples. "And how do you want it?"

"L-like," he pinched my peaks and tugged them down, "like this, Sir."

He rose up, nudging his cock between my pussy lips. "Like this?" The slow guide stretched my inner walls.

Then, his crux, that appendage at his base that brought me so much pleasure, kissed my rosebud. Brok paused. "And here?"

*Oh fuck.* I'd never taken anything there before. Never even thought about trying it. But with his cock half way inside me, and his crux poking my backside, I wanted it. "Yes."

He hummed his approval. Then, he circled around to my clit, withdrawing his cock. I cried out at the loss. "Shh, my Truxoria. Trust me," he crooned. Two thick fingers dove inside me once and pulled out, then his cock returned to my aching pussy. I felt those fingers circling my rosebud. Slowly and with infinite tenderness, he pushed those fingers coated with my juices inside me.

I groaned. The sensations were overwhelming. He used our intimate communication to reassure me, to tell me how brave I was, how beautiful as I opened to him. Then, he scissored his fingers in my ass, spreading me wider. When he withdrew them, I was shocked to find I wanted them back. "Sir, please."

"Yes, targana. You're ready now." He pushed his cock back inside my pussy, this time going past the halfway point. His crux breached my rosebud, and when his cock hit bottom inside me, I screamed my pleasure. I'd never felt so full in my life. He pulled out halfway, then thrust home. He kept his pace slow and easy, but I didn't want that.

I wanted everything.

"Give it to me, Brok." I tilted my head over my shoulder to look back at him. "I want all of it. I need it."

"As my mate commands." His thrusts turned harder, fucking me so good, I saw stars. Then, his cock and crux vibrated.

I screamed until my throat was raw. I gripped the sheets. I fell to my forearms and stuffed my face into the pillows. He claimed me with the force of a ship engine, and I loved it. I just needed a little more to reach the peak. Pushing his body over mine, he kept one arm at my hips to hold me steady, then the other to reach around me and rub my clit.

That did it. My pussy spasmed. My ass clenched his crux. He held fast inside me, the force of my release triggering his own. Hot seed filled my core and dripped down my inner thighs. With an arm around my waist, he guided me to lie on my side, his body tucked protectively around mine.

I sighed. I didn't know what news Brok's commander would bring us, and my mind stirred with the possibilities. But although I wondered why I couldn't simply talk to my fellow humans right away, there in my mate's arms, safe and sated, I just didn't care.

♄

I MUST HAVE DRIFTED OFF TO SLEEP, FOR WHEN I NEXT opened my eyes, I was wrapped in a blanket and a plate of food rested beside the bed.

Brok strode from the other room dressed in his leathers and a sleeveless black shirt. It was odd to see him in something beside his armor or bare chest. He sat on the edge of the bed and snagged the plate. "Hungry?"

I eyed the food with relish. "Starving."

We snacked on what my taste buds interpreted as a sort of chips and jelly combination. Odd, but not bad. When we'd cleaned the plate, Brok put it to the side, and handed me a water canteen and my now clean clothes. His words had a serious edge to them as he said, "The commander is ready for us."

"Oh." The food which had filled my empty belly now sunk like a stone in my gut. I pulled on my clothes as fast as I could and smoothed my hair, which had been cleaned by the goopy shower gel, back into a ponytail. "We'd better go then."

He stopped me with a hand on my shoulder and pulled me gently into his chest. "Whatever it is, Sage, we are in it together."

That pit in my stomach intensified, but I squeezed him around the waist. He was right. No matter what happened, we were a team. I nodded against his pecs, then turned, his hand in mine to face the music.

On the bridge again, the commander stood at the enormous viewer. He waved us to a side door when he saw us enter. The room had a large metal desk, with a chair on one side and a bench on the other, as well as a small viewer. Earth rotated on its axis below, the blue and green orb breaking up the blackness of space.

"Have a seat," the commander motioned to the bench. He didn't take the empty chair, instead he strode to the viewer, staring at Earth.

"Tell us what's going on, Tor." Brok led me to sit while he remained standing behind me, his hands on my shoulders for support.

I reached up and laid one of my hands over his. "Please, Commander. Why can't I talk with my friends?"

"You can, Sage." His wide chest shook as he exhaled deeply. "But I'm afraid things with Earth have grown more complicated."

I stood, alarmed by his words. "But I don't understand. Before I got blown into space, my sister said that the negotiations between your people and mine were going well." I shook off Brok's hands and paced the small room. I needed to move, to think. "Hell, our scientists discovered our genetic compatibility." My cheeks warmed as I thought just *how* well we fit together. "The government was going to broadcast your, um," I faltered a bit at how to frame their desire to find mates, but opted for, "marriage offer."

"They were," the commander said evenly. "But the attack by the Versaken has made your government uneasy." He ran a hand through his long hair. It had been tied back before, but now hung loose around his face. The strands were a thick black with streaks of silver shot through it. It gave him a distinguished yet wild look. He wasn't my type—only one male would ever be now—but he'd be another woman's fantasy, no doubt. His sigh was heavy. "I don't blame them."

"Tor," Brok headed toward the viewer, the chain of command breaking as he spoke as a brather, "it's not your fault. You're not responsible for their attack."

"No?" Pain was written all over the commander's face. "If not me, then who?"

Brok growled. "You have done all for our brathers. You carry this burden like a knife in your chest." He tapped his own chest, right between his hearts. "I know this pain. If you allow it to fester, it will consume you."

Not wanting to intrude but unable to be from my mate's side, I slowly walked to them and put a hand on Brok's back. He immediately tucked me under his shoulder and held fast. "This is what we fight for," he said motioning to me. "We are One. She and I. And our brathers deserve this chance too."

"Which is why we need an agreement with the Terrans." The commander folder his arms over his broad chest. "I," he blew out a shaky breath, "I am at a loss."

The defeat in his tone tore at my heart. "Let me talk to my sister. She'll know what to do." My stomach tightened in a knot. *If she's okay.* I hadn't let myself think of Jane and Taylor getting caught in the satellite blast. If something had happened to them, I would kill every last Versaken myself. So, they had to be okay. Nothing else was allowed.

"Who is your sister?" He tilted his head to the side.

"Captain Jane Kadaran." I smiled, picturing the face of my bossy but also total boss-babe big sister. "She's in charge of the moonbase."

The commander hesitated, letting his gaze move between us as if assessing the options.

Brok shrugged. "It can't hurt to try, Tor."

He walked to the bench, lifted it with one arm, and set it in front of the viewer. "No," the commander said, motioning for Brok and me to sit once more, "I suppose not." He stood off to the side, but with a clear view. "Activate communications." The viewer turned dark. "Sage, tell the ship who to call."

"Oh, um, call Captain Jane Kadaran." I watched as the viewer swirled in an array of bright pastel lines and then formed a video of my sister. I rose to my feet. "Jane?"

My sister screamed. "Sage! Oh my god. Am I hearing voices? What's going on?"

"No, Jane, it's me. I'm okay." I spun toward the commander in the corner. "Can she see me?"

The commander stood like a deer caught in the headlights of an antique vehicle.

Brok bade me sit and answered for him, "No, they don't have the technology yet. That's why your people kept getting fuzzy images of us." He took my hand in his. "But she can hear you."

"Sage!" Jane kept spinning around as if I'd appear in front of her. She was in her quarters on the moonbase. "Where are you?"

"I'll explain in a minute." A lump formed in my throat. "I'm just so glad you're okay. How's Taylor?"

"You think I'm okay? Sage C. Kadaran," she took on that mom-clone voice and I winced, "do you have any idea how worried we were? Taylor is fine but tearing apart every tech on this station to reroute it into a tracker for you." She swiped away the flyaway strands of her frizzy hair. "We thought you were lost forever."

"Jane, I swear I'm all right. I'll tell you everything. Can you get Tay to come to your room?" I leaned my head on Brok's shoulder seeking his strength. "It's kind of a long story. And we've got a lot to tell you. We need your help."

Swiping an instrument panel, I watched her send a message to Taylor. Then, her eyes narrowed as if she were looking right at me. "Little sister," she said so sweetly, "who is we?"

I gulped.

Taylor bounded into the room not five seconds later, saving me from an immediate answer. "Shit on a stick, Jane." She spun around as if searching for something. "Where is she?"

"Calm down, Taylor." Jane waved at her to take a seat. "Sage has messaged me but it's all audio. You'll hear her in a minute." She narrowed her eyes as Tay plopped on Jane's loveseat. "She's about to explain what the hell happened, and who this mysterious 'we' is that needs help."

"Oh, this I gotta hear." Tay leaned back and plopped her feet on the armchair.

"Hell," I mumbled. Then, I launched into my story—all of it. I started with my oxygen tank running to zero, which had Brok stiffening beside me, then I explained about the wormhole, the crash-landing, the dinolizard, flower-spiders, crab-giants, and our new friends, the gyorpins. Tay let out an, "aww," at their description. I told them about collecting the glava, the battle with the Versaken, and the fear that our enemies were amassing an army against Earth. I ended with the plight of the Rhonar and their need for Earth to cooperate on seeking mates. When I'd finished the rundown of events, I sprang the detail that I knew would drive the point home.

"And I understand how important mates are to them," I said, staring into Brok's eyes, "because I've found mine, and I'm never letting him go."

Tay choked on a candy stick she'd stolen from my sister's stash, and Jane jumped so high I was afraid she'd hit her head on the ceiling. They both started rattling off questions at once.

I laughed. "Ladies, I'll answer anything you want to know."

Brok cocked a brow at that.

"Well, almost anything." I held his hands in mine. "But first, we have some work to do. And I'll need your help."

He squeezed my palms and kissed my forehead. "*We* will need your help." The timber of his deep voice spoken to them for the first time made them both freeze.

Tay broke the silence. "Whoa Sage," her eyes widened and her mouth dropped open, "he sounds hot!"

Jane rolled her eyes. "I'll have some questions for you, um,…" she shot Tay a withering look and whispered, "what's his name?"

I laughed. "Brokdar," I supplied. "But call him, Brok. And he'll be happy to answer your questions too." Brok nodded at my declaration.

"Good." Jane blew out a deep breath. "But first, tell us what you need, Sage."

Tay rose to her feet to stand beside my sister. "Yeah, we've got you!"

And they did.

With my mate by my side, his brathers at our back, and my sister and friend on the job, we'd make this work. The Rhonar would claim their Earth brides, and us, Earth women? Well, we would claim our alien warriors right back.

Now, the real dilemma was how I was going to convince my big sister to be a bridesmaid. The answer? Only the stars knew.

# Epilogue
## TOR

"DRAV FEMALE!" I SAT UP IN BED, THE MOVEMENT scattering pillows to the floor. My cock rose beneath the sheet.

I groaned. Ever since I'd seen Captain Jane Kadaran on the viewer, my mind refused to think of anything else. I needed to concentrate on our problem and discover a solution to the tensions with Earth. I had to find a way to stop our enemies and end their wormhole technology. I was the commander of the Rhonar fleet. My warriors depended on me to lead them.

But my stubborn thoughts kept straying to *her*.

I was agitated, on edge, and while the void swirled inside me, need—incessant, ever-present, crexing need— gripped me. I took my cock in hand, picturing her face. Her untamed hair danced about her cheeks, as if, like the female herself, it could never be bound. Her skin was the hue of the Goldarin desert sands at night. Her eyes were a blue so deep, they shone like crystals in the Valar caverns. She reminded me of home, of a world I had not seen in too many orbits.

"Jane," I whispered her name in the darkness of my quarters. The shame of using her image to seek my release did not temper the lust. Nothing would. Not until I claimed her as my—

"Crex!" I shouted as I came. My seed spilled over the sheets, making a mess of it. I kicked them off the edge of the bed and headed for the cleanser.

The swirl of dim emotions inside me was enough for me to know the truth. Jane was...

I couldn't name the word aloud, nor even confess the truth in my own mind. To admit it would be to betray my brathers. For how could I take that which I failed to give? My brathers suffered, and if I did not find a path for them to claim their brides, then what right had I?

I stared into the reflector. It scanned me, projecting a three-dimensional image of my face. I looked tired, old, haggard. Where was the warrior who had led his people with grit and determination? The silver streaks in my hair had multiplied as if overnight. My body, through strong and heavily muscled, was tense at all times. The burdens of leadership weighed on me.

"Incoming transmission," the ship's voice intoned.

"Put it through. Audio only." I tied back my hair and used a wet towel to scrub myself clean.

A deep bass filled the room. "Tor," the male said without formality, "you're needed on the bridge."

My second-in-command, Galagar, was of my *Brather* and my oldest friend. He alone knew of my worries, but I had not told him the truth of my suspicions about the Terran captain. That I kept locked tight inside my chest. "I'll be right there."

Throwing on my leathers and my armor—a habit more than a necessity, although becoming more so with the Versaken prowling at out doorstep—I headed for the bridge. My warriors stood at their posts, their fists thumping their chests when I stepped on deck.

"What's the situation?" I took up the command post, next to my lieutenant.

Galagar handed me a pad. "Brok's mate has been studying the enemy's wormhole generator, and she believes she may have discovered how it generates the needed force."

I stared at the report of the wormhole generator on the pad. The Terran engineer had been busy.

"Her name is Sage." Brok grumbled as he strode through the doorway onto the bridge.

"I am aware, Brokdar," Galagar turned to him, "but I do you honor by naming her your mate."

The male's narrowed eyes said he didn't quite believe my first officer. But he did not comment further.

I handed the pad back. "This is good news, but not why you called me to the bridge." Although my abilities gave me insight into people in a manner no other Rhonar could understand, I knew Galagar well enough without such powers.

"No, Commander." He motioned to the viewer and said, "On screen."

Jane's face appeared. Her pert nose scrunched up. "Oh, it's working!" She stared at me as if seeing into my soul. "Wow, um, sorry." Pulling at the bottom of her buttoned-up jacket, she straightened and tilted her chin. "We've been trying to get it to work for a while. Didn't think it ever would." Clearing her throat, she continued, "Right so, proper introductions at last. I'm Captain Jane Kadraran, and I'm in charge of Earth's moonbase." Her voice was solid, firm as a leader's should be. "The Global Alliance of Nations has decided to suspend the announcement of the Rhonars offer to Earth women in light of the Ver——," she turned to someone off screen and whispered, "how do you say their name?"

I stepped forward, looming like a giant on the viewer. "It's Versaken, Captain Jane," I began, surprised to find my voice filled with gravel but otherwise steady, "and we understand your government's concerns. We will not allow them to attack Earth."

"Yes, well," her cheeks took on a darker hue that confused me, but before I could ponder it, she continued, "be that as it may, GAN's leaders has put an offer on the table."

My translator couldn't decipher the latter part of her statement. I ignored it, opting to focus on the important words. "An offer?"

She nodded. "As you know, they're allowing Sage to remain on board your ship for now as a," she paused a click as if searching for the right term, "personnel exchange." On Captain Jane's advice, Sage and Brok had not revealed their mating to Earth's government yet. With negotiations in jeopardy, the female feared it would "rock the boat" as she put it and endanger her sister. "That fosters good will. But they want assurances that the Rhonar can protect Earth."

My second-in-command interjected, "They doubt our prowess?"

A feminine squeak could be heard off screen, but the captain silenced her with a shh-shh sound. I was intrigued by the interaction. But watched the screen with careful eyes as she said, "No, but they need more. And since you promised to share your technology, our scientists have been studying the schematics of different," she winced as if she did not agree with her leaders but she did not allow it to stop her, "machines. And they want you to provide ergamite crystals to power a defensive system around Earth."

*Crex.* I cursed Miach for allowing him to convince me to share our tech with the Terrans. He wanted to give them medical abilities to help their injured and sick. I sighed inwardly. I couldn't fault him for that, and although I believed we were careful in what we shared, it was clear now we had not been vigilant enough. I captured the captain's attention and raised my voice to a near roar. "Ergamite is rare, and what you ask no small thing." I stared at her through the viewer. "It will not be easy to obtain."

Her nose twitched, but she held my gaze. "I am aware of the dangers, Commander. We did research the material from your archives."

She stood yet straighter as if she could somehow make herself appear more intimidating. I smiled at the display —it was a warrior's posture.

"You know nothing, little Terran." I baited her. It wasn't appropriate as one commanding officer to another, and yet, I could not stop from rifling her feathers. "Ergamite can be acquired only in the Meta Sector and through narrow channels. It will require a mission of finesse by skilled warriors." I scanned the room, considering who would be best for such a challenge.

"As I said, *Commander*," she emphasized my title, a hint of reprimand in her voice, "I've studied the situation, and I'm confident it can be done." Her arms crossed over her chest, and she breathed deep. "It's why I've volunteered for the mission."

My hearts stopped, both of them at the same damn time, and my mouth went dry. When I could find my voice again, I stammered, "You?"

She bristled. "Yes, me."

The little captain had spunk, fire, and it shot a bolt of lust down my spine. I scanned the room once more. If the Terran female insisted on taking this mission, then by Celestia's design, I knew what had to be done. "So be it, Captain Jane." I let my lips curl in a wicked smile and held her captive in the heat of my gaze. "If this is your desire, then," the words lingered on my tongue as they gained traction in the space between us, "we go together."

Thank you for reading! Did you enjoy? Please add your review because nothing helps an author more and encourages readers to take a chance on a book than a review.

Want a special **BONUS SCENE** of Brok making Sage his favorite dessert and serving it… on her? Then join my newsletter HERE for that upcoming bonus release, and all the latest sales, reveals, and giveaways!

And don't miss more in the Earth Brides & Alien Warriors series with book three, ALIEN'S TEMPTATION, available now! Will Captain Jane and Commander Tor survive their mission…together? Turn the page for a sneak peek!

This book has been edited and proofed. However, pesky

grammar gremlins are like space dust, you just can't get rid of it! If you would like to help fight the battle against them, however, please feel free to send them to AlienBookLover@gmail.com with the Subject Line: GRAMMAR GREMLINS.

Thank you and happy reading!

# Sneak Peek of Alien's Temptation
## JANE

I paced the corridor of the landing bay. As the captain of Earth's moonbase, the heavy burden of leadership laid on my shoulders. It was foolish to volunteer for this away mission and ask my first officer to bear the weight of command in my absence. Yet, I refused to send anyone else. I'd not dare put another in danger—and not with *that* alien.

"You know you're going to wear a hole in the floor, Captain." My first officer, Mai Sato, stood with her back to the wall—out of my walking path—and held a holo-pad in front of her. Her thick bangs fell over her forehead, but I was sure it was scrunched in thought as she tapped the screen. "I've put together a list of personnel shifts for your approval and uploaded the Rhonars' information regarding the Meta Sector to your personal device."

I halted mid-step and turned toward her. Holding out my hand wordlessly for the holo-pad, I waited until she looked up at me. "You know, Mai," I took it from her, signed the bottom without reading the list, and handed it back to her, "I'm not going to be in charge in the next ten minutes, you are." I kept her gaze locked with mine and squeezed her shoulder. "And I trust you completely. Have faith in yourself."

A small smile tilted her lips at the corners. "Yes, Captain."

"And thank you for the Meta Sector information." I tapped my holo-watch on my wrist and projected the files. I swiped through the folders, noting the names for later. "Does this include the details on the ergamite crystals we need for Earth's defense system?"

"It does." She tucked her holo-pad under her arm.

"Good." I closed the projections. The ergamite was the reason I was stuck in the landing bay, waiting for the arrival of the alien warriors and my sister. Sage, second in line of us Kadaran sisters after me, was an engineer on the moonbase. But after an attack on the satellite station, she was propelled into space.

Even now, the memory of that day was enough to send me into a cold sweat. I'd never been so scared in my life. Although losing people was inevitable in a field as dangerous as ours, the thought of one of them being my sister gutted me.

*She's okay. She's on our way here.* I clenched my fists at my sides in the present.

Thankfully, she'd been rescued by a Rhonar warrior, and through a bizarre series of events that I was still trying to wrap my head around, she ended up mated to him. We'd held their wedding in secret to avoid tensions between the aliens and us as negotiations between our species were…complicated. My younger sisters were already planning a larger second ceremony and party when a deal was finalized between our kinds.

And that's where the ergamite came into play.

Earth's government, the Global Alliance of Nations, would agree to allow the Rhonar to seek brides from our population, if, and only if, the alien warriors proved they could protect Earth. The ergamite allowed us to create and power a defense system, according to the aliens' shared technology, which would effectively surround the planet. The system, along with continued Rhonar presence in Earth's orbit, were non-negotiable terms.

*And it will protect Sage.* As much as I wanted to believe I was doing this for the good of our planet, my heart knew the truth. I'd do anything for my sisters, even change the laws of the universe to see them happy. *If the big lug is who she wants, then so be it.*

At that thought, the ship carrying said big lug, my sister, and an alien that I *really* didn't want to see again touched down in the landing bay. "Chin up, Jane," I muttered and readjusted my uniform jacket. "You do not let that bastard get under your skin again."

Mai graciously kept silent at my decree.

The Rhonar space fighter was a sleek triangular shape with a silver sheen to the metal and equipped with stealth shielding. Ships just like it patrolled our orbit in intricate flight patterns. I'd be lying if I said I didn't admire the design.

As the ship landed, Mai and I stepped forward to greet its occupants. But when the hatch opened, shouts from behind us caught our attention. "Wait! Wait!" Taylor, tech specialist aboard the station and Sage's best friend, came running. Both arms loaded down with bags, she dropped them when she reached us and sucked in fast breaths. "Whoa. I am not cut out for sprinting."

"Maybe not." Mai smiled at the shorter, curvier woman. "You're built more for strength than speed."

Taylor straightened, her pale skin flushing which made her freckles stand out, and her blond hair flipping back in its ponytail. She flexed her bicep and patted the muscle. "You know it."

Before I could respond, a short brunette with wide green eyes launched from the ship. "Taylor! Jane!"

"Hey peanut." I wrapped my sister up in a bear hug and swung her off her feet. No one who saw Sage and I together would ever guess we were siblings. Adopted by the world's greatest mom, and not being blood relations, we were polar opposites in appearance. I was tall and tan with blue eyes, a wide nose, and out-of-control hair, which my mother said was a blessing of my Polynesian heritage. I tended to disagree. Sage was short and fair with green eyes, a cute, pert nose, and easy to tame locks, which I envied.

Sage laughed, the corners of her eyes crinkling. "You haven't called me that in forever." Her head cocked to the side and her smile dropped. "You worried?"

"Me?" I let my shock coat the question. "Never."

"That's a lie." Taylor piped in, taking her turn for a hug, and whispering something in my sister's ear. "The captain has been beside herself since you've been," she cleared her throat, emphasizing her words, "away."

"Well now, it's you going away, sis." Sage popped me lightly in the shoulder and waved at Mai. "You ready to be in charge, Acting Captain Sato?"

Mai's brows rose to her hair line as she clutched the holo-pad to her chest. "Ah yes, Lieutenant."

"She'll be fine." I grabbed Sage's arm and brought her attention back to me. I couldn't keep the excitement from my voice as I asked, "Now, is this the ship for the mission?"

"It is *my* ship." A hulking alien warrior emerged from the hatch. His black hair streaked with silver was tied tight at the nape of his neck. Since he had to be seven-feet tall, I had to crane my neck to peer up at him. My jaw clenched at that fact. His purple rimmed gray eyes bore into mine. I kept my chin raised, refusing to glance again at his chiseled chest covered only by a black vest or his thick thighs clad in leather. The tattoos on his shoulders and biceps were metallic in nature, and as I'd learned from Sage, symbolized his family and his brathers. When mated, they'd flow to his forearms and wrists in a chosen pattern for his beloved as was the way of the Rhonar. Commander Torian's arms were noticeably bare—not that I was looking.

"Sister," the warrior behind him, who I liked infinitely better, walked around the sullen commander and held his arm out to me, "it is my honor to see you again."

Clasping Brok's forearm in their warrior's grip, I smiled up at my brother-in-law. "It's good to see you too. Have you been taking care of my sister?" It was a rhetorical question. Sage had called me almost every day while aboard the Rhonar ship to spill the details about her alien husband. I'd never heard someone more in love.

Brok's face grew solemn. "I will always do so." He clasped his fist to his sternum and bowed his head. "You have my word."

I placed a gentle hand over his where it rested above his double hearts. "I know, Brok. Thank you."

Out of the corner of my eye, I saw the Rhonar commander stiffen. His gaze narrowed at my hand on Brok, as if he wanted to chop it off. I pulled away as he barked, "No more delays. We need to leave."

"Already?" Sage turned her puppy dog eyes my way, and then to her mate.

"Commander," Brok tucked her under his arm and pulled her to his side, "could we not stay a few spans? Sage has been away from the Terran's moonbase for some time, and I'm sure she'd like to catch up with everyone."

Commander Torian crossed his arms over his massive chest. His booted feet stood wide. "And that is why you've been granted time off." A ghost of a smile appeared on his lush lips but disappeared so quickly, I thought I had to have imagined it. "We have not told the Terran government about your mating yet. And you must be careful not to reveal it while you're here beyond this present company. But their government has granted you a special dispensation." He handed Brok a com-storage that he pulled from his vest pocket. "Sage spent time with us, and now you will remain on the moonbase as part of our personnel exchange to better learn each other's cultures." The commander patted my brother-in-law's shoulder. "That is until I've returned from my mission."

"Our mission," I corrected quickly. *Give this alien an inch and forget a mile, he'll take the whole damn universe.*

Commander Torian dropped his grip on Brok and angled that steely gaze of his on me. "Yes, little captain, *our* mission."

I bristled. "It's Captain, or Jane, if you can be civil enough to treat me with the respect due to me."

A light emanated from his pupils turning the gray of his eyes to sparkling silver. That ghost of a smile slipped out too. "As you wish, *Captain*." He emphasized my title in a manner that set my blood on fire—whether from anger or…something else, I didn't yet know or want to think about at all. "As we'll be partners in this mission, you may call me, Tor."

"All right, then, *Tor*." I accentuated his name as he had with my title. Choosing to be the bigger person, I stuck out my arm. Distantly, I noted that my crew and brother-in-law were watching our exchange. I had to keep pace with the cocky commander. "So be it."

He stalked toward me, and I resisted squirming by a fraction. His gaze was intense—a predator staring down prey. But I was not so easily hunted. He'd learn not to underestimate me. I swore it. When my arm was within his reach, he grabbed my outstretched fingers instead of my forearm and brought my hand to his mouth. Slowly, he kissed each knuckle, my insides heating with the intimate touch.

I gasped and whispered, "What are you—"

Before I could get my bearings, he released me and stepped back. Spinning on his heel, he headed for the ship. "Hurry along then, little captain."

Flames leapt from my ears. They must have as the fire roaring inside me needed to escape. My cheeks were hotter than the sun. "You arrogant son of a—"

Taylor sprang up in front of me, the bags she'd been carrying earlier back in her arms. "Here! Look! I packed all the necessities." She transferred the bags to me, not giving me the time to properly unleash my fury. Sage came up on my right side and Mai on my left.

"I'm going to miss you so much." Sage wrapped her arms around the bags and me.

Mai waved the holo-pad like a flag. "Don't worry, Captain. I'll take good care of the base."

Releasing me, Sage sprang behind me with Taylor at her side. Each of them laid a hand on my back and pushed me forward. "Now, be careful, sis. And com when you can."

"No stress, Cap. We've got things covered," Taylor chimed in.

The infuriating alien stood at the top of the ship's platform with a smug expression on his face. I couldn't wait to wipe it off.

"Try not to kill him," Sage whispered in my ear.

I dropped my bags and tugged them each to my side, a one-armed hug for Sage and her partner-in-crime. "I know what you two are doing." I eyed my sister. "And I make no promises."

Taylor ducked under my arm to talk across me to Sage. "You want the under or the over."

"Oh, definitely the over." Sage squinted over my shoulder at the commander. "I give it a week."

The chuckles from them both had me shoving them away. I gave them each a pointed stare. "I don't even want to know."

Taylor smothered another laugh behind her hand. "I'll say five days."

"Bet," Sage said, shooting a loving grin in the direction of her hubs. "Then again, it might be less."

"No, no." A wagging finger from Taylor shot in the air. "A bet is a bet."

I picked up the bags and pointedly turned away from them. "I'm leaving now."

"Have a safe trip, Captain!" Mai called from the sidelines.

"Bye, Cap." Taylor waggled her eyebrows at me. "Be safe in all ways."

Sage slapped her arm. "You're bad." Waving a hand at me, she motioned toward the ship. "I can't hug you again or I'll start crying. So, get going and come back to us."

"Of course." I nodded and draped an arm around her one last time, despite her protests. I whispered to her, "Love you."

I felt a single tear against my neck before she swiped the rest away. "Love you too."

With no more to say, I picked up the bags that weighed a ton. *What the heck did Taylor pack in here?* I trekked up the ship's platform and through the lower hatch.

The commander waited with his arms crossed, his knee bent and one booted foot against the wall. He shot me a withering look. "Ready now?" He eyed my bags.

I hitched them higher in my arms. "Yes."

For a moment his arms extended as if he were going to take the bags from me, then he balled his hands into fists and whirled away. "Then, let's go."

"Fine by me." I rolled my eyes. Chivalry had died a long time ago on Earth, and that was when our population wasn't ninety-percent female. I didn't need anyone to save me, let alone some cranky alien.

"Hurry it up," he barked. His long legs ate up the distance.

I had to take two steps for every one of his. "You know…" I tightened my grip on the bags, fighting the urge to toss them at his head. "If you're going to be an asshat, this is going to be a long trip."

He snorted as he led the way to the bridge. Well, it was more like a cockpit with just two seats and a screen. But the panel in front housed a wide variety of controls that I was itching to learn. "Sit there," he pointed to the co-pilot's chair, "strap in, and don't touch anything."

"Might I remind you, I *am* a captain." I dropped the bags into a storage compartment and plopped in the chair.

He strapped into the pilot's seat and swept his hands over the console. "And might *I* remind *you* that I am in charge of this mission."

"What gave you that idea?" A deep, sardonic laugh bubbled from my chest. "This is a joint mission. Technically, the first between our species." I placed my fists above the control panel, daring him to say something. "We're equals."

His eyes shot daggers at me. "And do you know how to fly this ship, little captain?"

I flicked my gaze to his hands, then to the controls, and back again. "Not yet. But give me a few hours, and I will."

"Will you now?" The big jerk began the takeoff sequence with rapid movements.

I rose to his challenge, watching every move. No matter if a flipping meteor struck us, the Versaken attacked us, or a star imploded next to us, I was not taking my eyes off the controls. "Yes," I hissed between my teeth, "I will."

Don't stop now. Keep reading with your copy of
ALIEN'S TEMPTATION.

And if you'd like to connect about the Earth Brides &

Alien Warriors series with other readers, I'd love to have you join my Reader Group.

Want even more behind-the-scenes access with exclusive content, spicy art, steamy scenes, special discounts, and more? Check out my Patreon for all the details.

**Don't miss book three, ALIEN'S TEMPTATION,
for pre-order now, and discover more from
Tina Moss at www.tinamoss.com**

I'm the captain of Earth's moonbase. I can handle any mission. I do not need a partner, even if he is a sexy-as-sin alien commander, who looks at me like he's trying to decide between throttling me or…something else.

His grumpy demeanor and dominant streak make me want to shake him, but I can't deny the heat between us. Do I dare put my hand to the flame? I've been burned before. And I've guarded my heart ever since.

As we travel to a distant planet to find the rare substance that will save both our kinds, we soon discover the inhabitants have some odd customs. And if we don't follow their sensual mandates, they'll withhold the bounty.

The survival of the Earth-Rhonar treaty depends on our success. We can't afford to fail. But when victory depends on a death-do-us-part bond, can I put my heart on the line and trust again? And will this alien warrior lower his defenses to let me?

Only the stars know.

# Acknowledgments

Well, here we are again. Another marathon writing sprint to the finish line, and even though, the act of writing is often a solo endeavor, books would never take shape without the team's behind them. Thank you to mine.

To my hubs, thanks for being my alien hero. You may be from Earth, but you're every bit as alien to me! **grins** Thank you for the late night sacrifices of your beauty sleep, your endlessly entertaining writing "suggestions", and of course, your constant question of "how many more days until the deadline?" I appreciate your support, especially the tea. Always the tea.

To my family, who I told in not-so-subtle terms to please forget I existed for two weeks. Thank you for letting me disappear. Writing on deadline is exhausting. But I made it, so... call me?

To my ever and always, Granny Bird, thanks for always supporting me and beginning my journey and love affair with books. But...you can never read this one. Seriously, I can't survive that.

To my corgis, both my non-corporeal Chuck whose always with me, and to my little one Bear whose *really* always with me, like doesn't leave my side for a second with me, I love you to the moon and beyond. You are my happy place,

To my Fab Four, though smaller in number, we're greater in spirit. Thank you, Danielle Bannister, Sherri Hayes, and Marianne Morea for understanding my frantic cancellations and re-arranging of the podcast schedule. And only giving me minor crap for doing this marathon writing nightmare…twice.

To my Patrons and Reader Group lovelies, who indulge this author's weird shenanigans, thank you! You let me be who I am, and give boundless help and advice on all things alien romance. From the florin colors to the Rhonar phrases, you are very much a part of this book.

And last, but always first, to my readers. I hope these stories allow you to travel amongst the stars. May you get lost in the pages and dream of a sexy alien warrior all your own. Remember always that you are deserving, you are valuable, and you are loved. Thank you for your reviews, your emails, your comments, and your outpouring of support. It means more than you know. Until the stars align, and we meet again!

# About the Author

TINA MOSS s a USA Today Bestselling Author of urban fantasy, paranormal romance, and sci-fi romance. She lives in NYC with a supportive husband and corgi Bear, though both the males hog the bed and refuse to share the covers. Her corgi Chuck now lives in her heart. When not writing, she enjoys reading, watching cheesy horror flicks, and traveling. As a 5'1″ Shotokan black belt, she firmly believes that fierce things come in small packages.

www.tinamoss.com